DEATH
AT THE
CUT

DEATH AT THE CUT

DOUGLAS KIKER

RANDOM HOUSE

NEW YORK

Library of Congress Cataloging-in-Publication Data
Kiker, Douglas.
Death at the cut.
I. Title.
PS3561.I366D4   1988   813'.54   87-43220
ISBN 0-394-56952-0

Manufactured in the United States of America

2 3 4 5 6 7 8 9   9 8 7 6 5 4 3 2   2 4 6 8 9 7 5 3

First Edition

To Diana

I *know*. But, no.
Everything is imagination,
I tell you.

DEATH
AT THE
CUT

1

H E HAD ELUDED ME for years and I was determined to get him this time. I had spotted him, positive I had, the day before, when I was walking along the shore of Clam Pond, a square-inch flash of bright yellow, a swatch of lemon patched to pitch-black, spotted him and spent the rest of the day in preparation.

I poked around in the garage at the old unoccupied house next door and found just what I needed, three rusted screened doors, so all I had to buy was four hinges, some sort of camouflage netting and a camp-stool. I got the hinges at North Walpole hardware, which didn't stock campstools, no call for them. But the musty garage also provided the answer to that, a wooden chair with its spoked back cleanly snapped off. No doubt a story in itself.

The big problem was the netting, which I had to have to stand any chance of success. I was almost broke, what else is new, but I threw budgetary caution to the winds, bought two knotted white cotton twine Mexican hammocks at Brouse Around, a gift shop that had just opened for the summer season, and two packages of Ritz dye, a dark green and a brown, at the Alden variety store on Main Street. I dyed the hammocks in a laundry sink in the basement and they came out more or less olive green, close enough. "What in the world are you doing?" Kate asked me when she saw the soppy hammocks laid out on the lawn to dry in the late May sun. It was a warm day for that time of year on Cape Cod.

"A secret passion from my past life," I told her. "It's called *Spinus tristus* in Latin. I'm going to need your help."

When I explained my plan she rolled her eyes and said, "Oh, boy." She had blue-green eyes, blond hair, a lean and lanky body, a quick Irish temper and a sharp tongue. "One of these days, Alice," I said and shook a fist the way Jackie Gleason did it whenever she went too far with me, which was quite often. Kate never hesitated to let you know exactly where she stood.

I got up early and built my hideout, hinged and set up the doors in a standing U shape, draped the dyed hammocks over the top and sides, then scattered over them the residue of the last winter's yard fall, small limbs, leaves, old and brittle bird's nests. With a pair of rusty garden shears I also found in the garage I cut narrow slits at eye level in the door screens, then took a seat on the backless chair and wondered how long its wobbly legs would hold me. I was ready, more or less.

4

At nine o'clock straight up, right on time and according to my plan, Kate walked out of the house with the dog MouMou close by her side and strolled across the lawn, down to the shore of Clam Pond, where I had set up my blind under a small grove of trees beside a concrete birdbath.

"Here I am!" she shouted. "I think I'll go inside this tent, or whatever it is." She threw back the flap of hammock and crawled inside with me. The dog MouMou, left outside, barked furiously at us. "Here I am, inside here!" Kate shouted.

"Be serious, will you?" I whispered.

"This is ridiculous," she whispered back.

"Birds can't count."

"You think I don't know that?"

"So when you and MouMou leave, they'll think nobody else is left here. An old trick, but it works. I see you brought some coffee. Thanks."

She gave me the thermos bottle and a small brown bag. "Also, a peanut butter sandwich. Can you see anything through those slits with those dime-store glasses of yours?"

"You're one to talk." Without her contacts, beautiful Kate was as blind as a hoot owl at high noon.

"I think I've got some good news for you," she said and gave me a pat on the cheek.

The dog MouMou growled at me, her dim and red-rimmed eyes ablaze with hatred because we were sworn enemies, this dog and I. She was sixteen years old and about the size and weight of a six-pack of assorted breakfast cereals, an old white poodle bitch, fragile and self-willed, that my wife, Earline, you heard that right, had dumped on me when she and I split. MouMou was Kate's dog now, would not leave her side. It had been that way since the day they met, five months before.

"So I'm waiting," I said. "Aunt Gloria finally passed on and the fortune's finally mine, right?"

"There was a call for you just before I left the house. Somebody named Terrell. He said to tell you you have a firm go-ahead. What does that mean?"

"He's an editor with the *New York Times Magazine*. It sounds like they're interested in an article I suggested."

"Okay. Good news."

"About time for some."

"Don't be such an old grouch." She looked at her watch. "I've got to go to work." Kate was executive director of the North Walpole Preservation Society and one of the directors of the huge private trust that funded it. Her office was in the library of the house in which we lived, so to get to work all she had to do was walk back home. "How long do you plan to sit out here?" she asked. "All day or what?"

"Until my patience runs out, which means probably not very long."

"Are you positive you actually saw the thing? Your eyes are going on you, Mac. I've warned you about that. Not that you ever listen to my advice."

6

"Get out of here, Kate. And make plenty of noise on the way."

She crawled out of the blind and stood up. "Come on, MouMou. We're leaving now! And there's nobody else here! Mac's certainly not here!" She and the dog walked away without looking back and I settled in.

I told myself I was prepared to wait all morning if necessary. It was a beautiful Cape Cod day, with blue skies and sunshine, although it was still a little chilly this early in the day, especially under the shade of the trees. The Cape doesn't really warm up until mid-June, or even later. So I had been told.

I ate the peanut butter sandwich and drank the coffee. I wished I had worn warmer clothing. After thirty minutes I admitted to myself I no longer had the patience required to be a bird photographer. I longed for a cigarette and I prayed for my *Spinus tristus* to come.

I had set up and leveled my wooden tripod inside the blind at a height that gave my camera lens a clear, unobstructed view through the slits I had cut in the screening. It was a Nikon F3 frame, solid as a rock, with a 200–600-millimeter zoom lens, and I had loaded a fresh roll of ASA 64 Kodachrome film, which I had found to be the best for color prints.

I had scattered cracked corn, raisins and sunflower seeds on the ground around my blind and tacked a few orange slices to the lower branches of the trees.

I'm a bird hunter, grew up as one in small-town Illinois, and a good one. When I was a teenager I could not imagine a more pleasant way to spend a free autumn day. I don't hunt animals, only birds, and that had led me into amateur bird photography. I like to spend time alone in the woods, used to be a fanatic about it, until I got married to Earline and became involved in other things on weekends, shopping at malls, paying bills, home repair, interesting things like that. This was my first shoot in years.

At eleven o'clock, after two hours of waiting, my patience—what little was left—was partially rewarded when chickadees, then bluejays showed up around the blind. Next came sparrows, grackles and a single redwing blackbird. They ate the corn. A pair of cardinals came and ate the raisins. A Baltimore oriole flew in and helped himself to one of the orange slices, so pretty I took his picture even though I already have terrific oriole shots. Lots of birds, but no *Spinus tristus*.

The American goldfinch is a wild canary that sings a soft, sweet song and builds its nests with thistle. In the spring the male has a vivid yellow back, black wings and tail feathers, and a tiny black cap perched on its crown. A beauty, and a bird that was missing from my collection.

My name's McFarland, first name Horace, which I don't answer to, and I'm a newspaperman, a reporter who spent twenty-five years on a Chicago daily until I was canned by the new owner, whose blood, sex and scandal approach to the news of the day didn't exactly match my own concept of responsible journalism.

The garage where I discovered the screened doors was part of a drafty old barn of a house where I had lived in a half-frozen state the previous winter after I had wandered onto the Cape, broke, burned-out and despondent, on a wild exodus from a failed life.

I had been offered a new job as a staff reporter for the Boston *Globe*. I do have a good national reputation in the business, won a Pulitzer, and the editors at the *Globe* had been pleased by the work I had done for them as a temporary stringer, reporting the murder of a rich old woman named Jane Drexel. But it would have meant moving to Boston, so I turned the job down. Because I had met Kate and Kate wouldn't go to Boston. By love possessed, that was me. Also, unemployed and at loose ends.

Now, at least, I had the *Times Magazine* assignment, which should bring in three thousand or so. I'd ask for three and take two, fifteen hundred if it came down to it. The fact was, I needed the work as much as I needed the money, which was a lot.

The subject of my proposed article was Adolphus Bridges, one of the hottest presidential prospects the Republican party had at the moment. Bridges was in his mid-fifties, four or five years older than I, a handsome, dynamic, moderate-conservative who had served two six-year terms as the United States senator from Illinois. He

9

then had declined to run for certain reelection to a third term because he wanted to run for president instead.

The modern presidential nominating process that has evolved in recent years, with the proliferation of state primaries and party caucuses and new federal campaign finance rules, has become so complicated and time-consuming that it must be approached by any serious candidate as a full-time job these days.

It would be another full year before the political parties would hold their nominating conventions, but Dolph Bridges was already making plans. He was holed up in North Walpole, away from the Washington heat in a summer home owned by his national finance chairman. He and key members of his campaign staff were developing strategy and tactics for the crucial months to come, and it was my hope that these planning sessions, being held before the pressures mounted and Bridges's schedule became more crowded and frantic, could provide the setting and background for my profile. If he made it, there might even be a book in it for me. I had an appointment to see him the next day.

I had known Dolph Bridges since 1968, when I covered his first campaign for federal office, a congressional race in the Illinois Twelfth District, northwest metropolitan Chicago, Waspy, affluent and heartland conservative. He and Richard Nixon both won handily there that year. In my letter of proposal I told the editors at the *Times Magazine* about this old connection—okay, maybe exaggerated it a little—and I suspected that was one reason I had been given the assignment. Coattails, and who doesn't need to catch a ride on them now and again?

Meanwhile, there was my bird to think about.

I kept looking around the yard. Kate was correct. My eyes were beginning to go on me. Just age. I woke up one morning and couldn't read the newspaper, next week couldn't read the phone book. The pair of nonprescription reading glasses I bought off the rack at the Alden variety store seemed to do the trick well enough, but Kate was leaning on me to drive to Hyannis, twenty-odd miles down Route 6, and have my eyes properly examined by an ophthalmologist. And maybe I would, after the Bridges profile had been completed and I had the money in my pocket to pay the doctor.

I could see perfectly well through my camera lens, however, could see, dimly, almost a mile away, and I kept zooming it in and out as I panned the Nikon on its tripod. I bought the camera and the lens from a news photographer in Chicago who was retiring, a bargain at three hundred and seventy-five during the days when I had a little cash in my pocket.

Had I really spotted a goldfinch? Or was he a dream bird, the by-product of boredom and inactivity on the part of Cousin Weak Eyes here? I wasn't sure.

I looked at my watch. Eleven-thirty now. A beer would taste good. I decided to give it another thirty minutes and then say to hell with it. I had work to do, after all, an article to put together. Before I made my proposal to the magazine I read up on Dolph Bridges in the town library, but now the time had come to do some heavy research. I wanted to be well prepared when I sat down with him the following day.

Clam Pond is a shallow saltwater inlet, part of North Walpole's Pilgrim Harbor, like a lump on the side of a boy's round head. The harbor is connected to Nantucket Sound by a narrows called the Cut.

I searched slowly around the shorelines of both the harbor and the pond with the camera, hoping to spot some telltale sight of yellow I could zoom in on and bring into proper focus. I no longer anticipated success, was only serving out my time. I don't respect people who give up on things without an honest try.

There. No, it was yellow junkweed in the yard on the opposite shore of the pond.

There. No, a short yellow slicker worn by a commercial clammer who stood in his boat in the middle of the harbor, tugging at his bullrake.

There. A man on a small yellow yard tractor, mowing his lawn.

There? Jesus, with a deep sigh. I was looking beyond the harbor, through the Cut, at a yellow trapboat working the fish weirs. I adjusted the focus and I could see the fishermen scooping up mackerel and butterfish with dip nets.

To hell with it. I'd walk back to the house, have a beer

and a tin of herring with some crackers and a little mayonnaise, then I would drive to the library and get to work.

There! In the Cut. What was it? Not a goldfinch. But something yellow. The camera lens was not quite powerful enough. It was submerged, whatever it was, just under the surface of the water, only a few feet away from the waterfront restaurant there. I fiddled with the lens focus again. Jesus Christ! Still not clear, but it looked like a car, a yellow car in the water.

I crawled out of the blind and ran across the lawn to the house.

2

I RAN THROUGH THE HOUSE shouting to Kate on my way. "Call the rescue squad! Call Noah! There's a car in the water off the pier at Cranberry House!" I didn't wait for an answer.

I jumped into my old Ford station wagon, shot out of the driveway and turned right on Clam Pond Drive, wheels and slick tires screeching and shimmying in strain and protest. A couple of hundred yards down the road, kids lined both walkways of the short wooden drawbridge that spanned the narrows joining Clam Pond to Pilgrim Harbor. They were fishing, after a fashion, trying to pull up a flounder, size being of no consideration, to drag home to Mom, for her to praise, clean and cook.

The older children and the fathers of the younger ones shouted in protest and shook their fishing rods at me when I went bounding across the slats of the bridge, moving far too fast.

I had no choice. Unless my failing eyes had deceived

me, I had spotted an automobile underwater at the Cut and I didn't know how long it had been there. Somebody might still be trapped inside it. Was I the first person to spot it? I didn't know. So I went roaring down the road as fast as my old car would take me, honking my horn at the turns and curves, and praying a lot because my horn worked only about half the time, when it was in the mood.

I was lucky because traffic was light. Cape Cod's full summer season was still a couple of weeks away. One last hard left and I was heading down the southeast shore of Pilgrim Harbor, toward the Cut, on a narrow two-lane asphalt road that dipped and rose over sand dunes like a carnival roller coaster.

From my position on Clam Pond I had seen the Cut clearly enough through my camera lens, but getting there in a car was a different matter because I had to follow the meandering waterline around the harbor, crossing small bridge after bridge that spanned saltwater creeks and marshes. It was ten minutes before I pulled into the pebbled parking lot of the restaurant, scattering stones when I skidded to a stop.

Cranberry House was, by reputation, including a glowing review by Marian Burros of the *New York Times*, one of the very best restaurants on the Cape. Certainly it was the most expensive in North Walpole. People who could afford the prices, rich summer people, came from miles around to eat there. Dinner for two with a couple of drinks and wine could set you back a hundred and a quarter plus tip, and you had to book a reservation two weeks in advance for the privilege. So I had been told. I'd never set foot inside the place myself.

The restaurant sat on the shore of the Cut, so called because it was an abrupt break in the shoreline of the Cape, like a missing front tooth, through which the tidal waters of the sound flushed into and out of the harbor. It once had been living quarters for the keeper of the Pilgrim Harbor entrance light, which still stood a few yards away, isolated, automated, fenced and untended, 8 Sec. Occ. on the navigation charts. Its close, sweeping lume the restaurant's guests now found magical and romantic, especially on foggy nights.

The new owner, a New Yorker named Nat Loory who was a friend of Kate's, had gutted and rebuilt the place and surrounded it with a treated pine plank deck where tables, chairs and umbrellas were placed for summer outdoor drinking and light dining, a nice joint, I'd been told, with a grand view of both the harbor and the sound, if you could afford the prices.

A sign posted in the parking lot said Cranberry House would reopen on Memorial Day weekend, featuring *As Always Simply Wonderful Food*! But now the place was shuttered and closed and, I noticed, one section of the railing that separated the deck from the water was shattered and broken.

I jumped out of my old Ford, ran over and looked down.

No, my eyes had not been playing tricks on me. There was a car down there, sitting on a clear, sandy bottom under three or four feet of water. No bubbles, nothing. It looked as if it had been there for hours, a mustard-yellow VW, a Beetle.

I jerked off my shoes and dived in, not knowing what I was going to find, thinking *This is where the goldfinch led* as I hit the water.

The door on the driver's side was open and the car was filled with water. The driver's seat was empty, but there was somebody in the front passenger's seat, a woman, wearing a seat belt. She had on a halter top and a cotton wraparound skirt, and her long straight black hair floated lazily around her face. Her mouth was open, her eyes closed.

I swam around, opened the passenger door—it wasn't locked—unfastened the seat belt, and pulled her out of the car by her hair. Then I hooked my left hand under her chin and, with three or four frogleg kicks, brought her to the surface.

There was a landing ladder, a few slats nailed to a piling, and I swam to it and dragged her up to the wooden deck, not an easy job because her body was limp.

I flopped her on her belly, face to one side, brushed her wet hair from around her face and reached inside her mouth and pulled her tongue out. Wasn't that what you were supposed to do? It had been thirty-five years since I had taken a lifesaving course. Back in the olden days. Okay, I was also a little winded and a little frantic. I could have kicked myself for not having enrolled in one of the emergency lifesaving courses they offer everywhere these days. Just never got around to it, like so many other things.

I straddled the woman and pressed my open palms against her rib cage. Let the bad air out, let the good air in, I remembered. I pushed harder and a little water gurgled out of her open mouth. But she was dead as a goldfish floating in a toilet bowl, clammy, totally lifeless, as cold as any stone.

Keep at it. Don't give up. I remembered they taught us that, and I was still at it, and still getting no response, when Noah Simmons arrived, pulled into the restaurant parking lot in his new Ford Fairlane police special, jumped out and ran over—an event, the way the aircraft carrier *John F. Kennedy* coming into view making flank speed is an event, because the police chief of North Walpole weighed three hundred pounds, most of it muscle.

He wasted no time. "How long?"

"I've had her out about five minutes. How long she was in the water I have no idea."

He glanced at the car in the water. "Anybody else in there?"

"No."

"Any response from her?"

"She's dead, Noah. At least, she feels dead."

"Get off her. Quick, move!"

Noah turned the woman over, held her in his huge

18

arms, and tilted her head back. He put his mouth to hers and breathed quickly into her mouth four times. Next he placed his fingers on her neck, to the right of her Adam's apple.

"I don't get a pulse," he said to me. "We'll do CPR. Get down by her head, Mac." He laid her on her back, straddled her and placed both hands on her chest. "I'll compress. You breathe in. Five to one. Here we go. One, one thousand. Two, two thousand . . ."

I held the woman's head cradled in my hands, and after every fifth compression Noah made I placed my mouth to her dead lips and blew air into her lungs. We kept it up for I don't know how long because you lose track of time doing CPR, kept it up until the big North Walpole rescue squad truck roared up and three paramedics took over. They had, and they tried everything, a defibrillator, a heart drug with an IV, more CPR, everything. And nothing worked.

"Kate called," Noah Simmons said as we stood to one side and watched the paramedics work. "I wasn't ten minutes away from here when I got the word over my radio. Just cruising. How'd you get onto this, Mac?"

"Bird photography, an old hobby of mine. I was down by Clam Pond. I've got a big zoom lens and I spotted the car in it."

"So you drove here, jumped in and pulled her out, and started doing what they taught you to do in the Boy Scouts back in the days of knighthood."

"I didn't know how long the car had been in the water."

"You did the right thing."

One of the paramedics walked over. "Chief, she's had it, I'm afraid. Not the first sign of life so far."

"Call the medical examiner on your radio. But keep the CPR going until he gets here. No letup, sixty to the minute. Mac and I will take turns in relief. And a pretty damn good response time, Dorsey."

The paramedic grinned. "Twenty-two minutes, point to point."

"A great improvement. With a few more drills under your belt, you'll get even better."

"Jesus, Noah, give us a break, will you?"

North Walpole was too small to support a salaried fire department, so the rescue squad was part of the police and Noah was the boss. The truck could never move out on call fast enough to suit him.

"Was there anybody else around when you got here?" he asked me.

"Not a soul."

He walked over and inspected the broken railing, peered down at the car, then turned and inspected the deck. "The car's only out there three or four feet, so it wasn't going very fast when it went in."

"That's the impression I get."

Noah started undressing, stripped down to his boxer shorts, white with the words *Big Daddy* written all over them, a Valentine's Day present from his oldest daughter that I had ordered for her from a specialty shop in Chicago. Noah was a redhead, with freckles. His huge chest was covered with red hair. He opened the trunk of his car, pulled out a face mask and a pair of flippers, and donned them. "I'm going down and take a look for myself before we pull it out." And in he went, feet first.

He was like a big sleek seal in the water. I stood and watched while he swam around the car, inspecting it closely. He poked his head inside, took a look at the dashboard and the driver's seat, then surfaced for air. *"Iterum et multa dictebo,"* he said and went under again.

On this second dive he swam to the other side of the car, to the open passenger's door, wiggled inside, and when he surfaced a few moments later I knew the packet of papers he was clutching in his left hand had to be the contents of the glove compartment.

He climbed up the ladder and pulled off his face mask. "No wallet, no handbag that I could see. The key's in the starter, switch is on, emergency brake's off, transmission's in automatic drive. Somebody drove it right through the railing, into the water."

Noah sat on the deck and sorted through the sodden stack of papers he had brought up, insurance papers, owner's manual, a big stack of unpaid traffic tickets. "District of Columbia. Our nation's capital," he said. "Her name is Susan Jacobs, 415 First Street."

I walked over and took a good close look at the

21

woman's face. Dorsey was over her, compressing and sweating like a sumo wrestler. "My God, it's Susan what's-her-name," I said.

"Jacobs it says on the license. Susan Jacobs," Noah said.

"Noah, Kate knows her. She was over at the house. In that car."

I had no more than said it when Kate arrived at the restaurant in her new white Honda Accord. I ran over to her before she could get out of the car. She looked me over. "You're a mess. You okay?"

"Yes, just wet. But there's been an accident. A bad one."

She looked at the paramedics at work, then turned her head away. "It's Susie Jacobs, isn't it. I finally put two and two together after I thought about it. She was living here."

"She's dead, Kate. Her car went into the water. I spotted it through my zoom lens."

"She was just a kid, Mac."

"Sorry, Kate," Noah Simmons said. He had walked over to her car. The two of them were old friends who had grown up together in North Walpole. They were the same age, thirty-one, their birthdays less than a month apart.

"Noah, I barely knew her," Kate told him. "She was my college roommate's kid sister."

"How'd she come to be in town?"

"She showed up unannounced. What, Mac? Maybe three weeks ago. She knew I lived here, so she looked me up. Remember, Mac? She drove by the house to see me. She said she was bored with her job in Washington, so she walked out, determined to have one more summer at the beach. Except she needed work. And a place to live."

"And how many times have I heard that story," Noah said. Young people from all over flocked to the Cape in the summertime, often without bothering to inform their parents of their whereabouts. One of Noah's big jobs during the season was tracking them down.

"I called Nat Loory in New York and got her a job as a summer waitress here at Cranberry House. He also let her move into the bunkroom, even though the place is still closed."

The bunkroom was a big bedroom above the restaurant where Loory let four or five waitresses, college girls, live free of charge. A flight of outdoor stairs led up to it. I had never met Loory, but he and Kate were tight and she had told me a lot about him. He was an aging homosexual with dyed orange hair, a good food man and a good businessman, according to her. He owned a second restaurant in the Caribbean somewhere that was open only during the winter season.

"A pretty good deal for her," Noah said.

"Susie seemed happy with it. She was going to help set the place up for the season this weekend. Until then, she

23

told me, she was going to lie here on the patio and sun herself. Which is what she did, I guess. I never heard from her again."

"Well, she got a nice tan," Noah said, glancing at the body. "A pretty girl."

"A knockout. She always was, even as a kid. Black hair, green eyes and a great body," Kate said.

"Just a kid. Twenty-six, according to her driver's license."

"That would be right. No older. I remember I first met her the summer after my freshman year at Wellesley when I went to Chicago to visit Martha, my roommate. Susie was a teenager then, thirteen or so. The last time I saw her, until she showed up here, was during our college graduation weekend. She came with their parents, about sixteen or seventeen then. All I know about her since then is what Martha has told me, or written me."

"You and Martha Jacobs are still close?" Noah asked.

"We keep in touch. She went on to law school after college. Now she's a lawyer with some big firm in Washington. We talk now and then on her WATS line."

"Jacobs. Jewish?"

"Martha is. Susan was a hillbilly."

The medical examiner had arrived, an elderly man named Hamish Percival who, before retirement, had a distinguished career as a professor of pathology at Harvard medical school. He waved at us and proceeded to the body.

"What do you mean 'a hillbilly'?" Noah asked. "She was her sister."

"Susan was adopted. From somewhere in the wilds of West Virginia, according to Martha. After Martha was born, her mother couldn't have more children. Her parents decided she needed a kid sister to grow up with. So they got Susan."

"I've known lots of nice people from West Virginia," I said. "Cultured people, refined people. It's a fact that today many members of the West Virginia state legislature not only read but write."

"Susan was always different," Kate said without the slightest smile at my little joke. "She grew up on the north shore of Chicago, in the lap of luxury, and in a very cultured atmosphere. Martha's dad was a very successful commodities broker. And an opera buff. Her mother wrote book reviews for the Chicago *Daily News*. But Martha said Susan was born a hillbilly, with a wild mountain look in her eye. It was in her blood."

"Martha obviously didn't like her adopted baby sister very much," I said.

"She didn't dislike her. She simply couldn't cope with her. She told me once that Susie's real parents must have been a bootlegger and a coal miner's daughter."

"A wit like that, Martha must be great before a jury."

"I don't mean to put Susan down, Mac," Kate said. "I can't even bring myself to walk over there and look at her body. I'm simply telling Noah what Martha said to me."

"And you're being helpful, Kate," Noah said. "Please go on and disregard Mac's sensitive nature."

"Well. There was a tree in their front yard at home, a tree with thick low limbs. Martha said when Susie was six or seven she would climb up on it and sit there for hours at a time, staring southeast at Appalachia with this longing in her eyes."

"I can tell you what it is," I said. "Martha was smarter but Susan turned out prettier. Am I right? Most people envy looks more than they envy brains, and Susan had the looks."

"Martha tried to be a good big sister. I know she did because she used to talk to me a lot about it in college. The two of them were never in synch. Martha is a quiet, steady type. And Susan was a born hell raiser who was always in hot water for one reason or another."

"Such as?" Noah asked.

"A high school pothead. Always into her parents' booze. A dropout at Northwestern after her dad moved mountains to get her admitted there. She had her driver's license revoked for drunken driving. Two abortions. Which Martha arranged and paid for to keep her parents out of it."

"A normal girl coming of age in modern America," I said.

"Christ, go fish, Mac," Kate said.

Dr. Percival walked over to us. He was a thin man with a ruddy face and watery blue eyes, in his eighties. "I'm pronouncing her dead, Noah," he said.

26

"Any idea how long she was in the water, Doc?"

"Twelve hours? Twelve to eighteen, no more."

"That means she went in last night sometime."

"That would be my estimate."

"Thanks, Dr. Percival. I guess Dorsey can take the body to the Barnstable County morgue now. I'd like an immediate autopsy, if that's possible."

"I'll see what I can do."

Noah waited until the doctor left to attend to his business. Then he said, "A college dropout, a pothead, a teenage drunk who kept getting knocked up."

"That was Susan, I guess," Kate said with a sigh.

"Did she live with her sister in Washington?"

"God, no. Susan bummed around out West for a few years. Then, oh, about a year ago she moved to Washington from California. Martha helped her find work and an apartment, and loaned her money for a down payment on a car. But they never lived together. I told you, they were never in synch, Noah."

"Was there anything unusual about her behavior the day she came to visit you? Anything about her that struck you as funny, or strange? Any evidence of drug use? Did she seem to be under any pressure? Anything at all? Did she mention any names, for instance?"

Kate thought about it. "No."

Dorsey gave a toot on his air horn as the rescue truck pulled out of the parking lot.

"The way she was dressed," Noah said. "It's not as if she'd been out anywhere. Barefoot, no bag, wearing a halter top and an old wraparound skirt. Dressed to hang around here, you might say."

"I've got to get in touch with Martha," Kate said.

"What about her folks?"

"Both dead. They died two years ago, within six months of each other. Martha's the only living relative."

"Get her up here. I need to talk to her. Right now, I'm going to take a look at the bunkroom. I don't want anybody else up there. Then I'm going to put a police lock on the door, seal it, and send for a forensic team from the state crime lab in Boston."

"I don't understand," Kate said.

"She'll get it out of me when we get home," I told Noah. "You know how she is."

"Tell her, then. But I don't want her sister, Martha, to know any of this, not yet. Remember that, Katie."

"Kate, I found Susan's body in the passenger's seat, not in the driver's seat. Seat belt fastened. And Noah doesn't believe she drove her car into the water, then crawled over into the passenger's seat, fastened her seat belt, and sat there and drowned."

"No, I don't subscribe to that theory."

"You think she was murdered?" Kate asked.

"I don't know that," the young police chief said. "I do think somebody else was driving that car."

3

I CALLED THE BOSTON *Globe* and dictated five para-
graphs on the death of Susan Jacobs, identifying her
as an employee of the federal government whose home
was in Washington, then spent the rest of the afternoon
at the public library, reading and taking notes on the life
and career of Senator Adolphus Branford Bridges,
helped by a bright-eyed, blue-haired volunteer assistant
who couldn't have been more kind.

Day's work completed, I escorted her down Main
Street to the municipal parking lot. A few summer residents had arrived in North Walpole and the tempo of the
little town was quickening. There was more traffic on
Main Street, and parking places, a given during winter
months, were hard to spot. But it was still early in the
season, still too cold to hit the beach, still too chilly to
sail or boogyboard. Private schools were still in session.

Cape Cod is an air-conditioned peninsula, shaped like
a cocked arm, which stretches into the North Atlantic off

the Massachusetts coast. June, July and August are the only three months when the town of North Walpole becomes Standing Room Only, the months when affluent people from other places, Boston, New York, Washington, find the summer heat at home intolerable and come there, seeking relief.

At the Binnacle bar and grill, Mary Beth, the waitress, spotted me the moment I walked inside. "You're the first to arrive," she said. "Nickey's saving places at the bar."

Mary Beth was Noah Simmons's niece, a child-woman of twenty-one who had long black hair and tits that, had they been melons, would have won first prize at any state fair. She was wearing wheat jeans and a black T-shirt that said *Once Is NOT Enough* across its front.

At the bar, Nickey, the owner-manager, drew me a draft Narragansetts without asking. He was wearing a yellow button-down shirt, a bow tie and a straw boater.

"You got a walk-on in a remake of *Meet Me in Saint Louis*?" I asked. "Is that it?"

"For the summer tourists. All the help starts wearing the outfit tomorrow."

"It adds real class."

Kate and Noah walked in, spotted me and came to the bar. Nickey pulled two more drafts.

"Where's Bascombe? Has he chickened out?" Noah asked.

"Bascombe called," Nickey said as he served the beers. "He said to tell you he's been held up but he's on his way."

"And I happen to know he's bringing a new weapons delivery system with him," I said. "We're going to blow the both of you out of the water today."

"Bascombe's worse than you are. If that's possible," Kate said.

"We'll see. We'll just see about that. I know for a fact that my partner has put in long hours this week practicing at home *and* at his office. Hour after patient hour."

"Here he comes," Kate said.

"His usual martini," I told Nickey.

The lawyer Bascombe Midgeley, always a natty dresser, was wearing a dark gray suit, complete with a vest, white button-down oxford shirt, a paisley bow tie, and round gold-rimmed glasses. A Phi Beta Kappa key dangled from the gold watchchain strung across his belly. It was genuine. He had thin stringy hair, which tended to fall over one side of his face, and he was a little overweight. Bascombe was a young man who was full of himself, even a little pompous, but, I had learned, also far more intelligent and tougher than he appeared at first to be.

He arrived at the Binnacle that afternoon carrying a new dart board under one arm. "Take that ratty thing off the wall and mount this beauty in its place," he told Nickey, handing him the board with a satisfied smile. "I've had more than enough points stolen by Noah and Kate in past contests because of obscured lines."

Nickey whistled. "That's a beauty. Thanks a million, Bascombe."

"Don't be absurd, Boniface. This is for our exclusive use. Genuine boar's bristle. It cost me fifty dollars at Abercrombie and Fitch. When the four of us stop playing, down it comes, and the old one goes back up. You can store this one in the back somewhere for us."

We were a gang of four that winter and spring, Kate, Noah, Bascombe and I. We played darts for drinks every Wednesday afternoon at the Binnacle, from six until seven, and Nickey always reserved the board for us.

During the winter months the Binnacle was the only bar open in North Walpole. It was the town's afternoon and evening hangout until late May, when other places opened for the summer season and bored regulars drifted away in search of a little badly needed variety. "Never mind, they'll all be back next fall," Nickey said, and he was right.

"Old cock, hold your breath," Bascombe said to me after Nickey had mounted the board. He pulled a small box from his coat pocket and opened it with a flourish. Three new darts. "Mac, they are to die over," he whispered. "Accudarts. Nickel-silver alloy. Modified to my own specifications with Darrow Flight Tips. One simply can't miss with these, old cock. One simply closes one's eyes and throws away."

"That's not fair!" Kate cried. "Noah and I get to use them, too."

"Go fish, my dear," Bascombe said airily. "And let the weekly competition begin."

32

We played 501, strictly by official English rules. Bascombe had a book and he turned to it frequently whenever there was any dispute. You had to throw a double in the narrow outer circle of the board to start subtracting points from 501 and you had to throw a double precisely equaling the final number of points to go out. There is not all that much to do on the Cape that time of year, so the four of us had gotten pretty good at the game.

This turned out to be a close one. Now and again I would get hot and couldn't miss, but I really was the weakest player of the four of us, and never worse than that afternoon. Bascombe had a magic arm, however, and with a series of great shots that made up for my erratic ones, he brought us quickly down to his favorite winning double.

After he shot, he rushed to the board and retrieved the darts so Kate couldn't get at them, then handed them to me. "Thirty-two. Piece of pie. Give me that double sixteen, a shot these two upstarts will long remember."

My first two shots were wide and the third was a single sixteen.

"You blew it, Mac, blew it as usual!" Kate cried happily.

"Hard cheese," Bascombe muttered. His next time up, he missed the double eight but got a single, which meant I had to make a double four, high on the upper right side of the board and very difficult for me. I missed it. *"Drat!"* Bascombe said.

Held in Noah Simmons's huge right hand, a dart looked like a toothpick. He and Kate were sitting on fifty points.

"Show them how the big boys do it, Noah," Kate whispered.

He did. He hit a thirteen, then, wham, bam, a triple five and a double eleven. Kate screamed and hugged his neck.

I thought Bascombe was going to faint. His face was flushed. "Don't you dare try to tell me that was skill!" he shouted. "Blind, dumb luck, that is what that was, sir."

"Visio recta, manus constans, cor fortis."

"And knock off that mumbo jumbo."

"Just think, Noah made those fifty points with old ordinary house darts," Kate said. "Think what he could have done if he'd been throwing Accudarts with Darrow Flight Tips. He'd probably have scored a hundred and fifty points."

"Fish, Kate. Fish, fish, fish."

Bascombe bought the round of drinks and we took a time-out. It was a comfortable feeling for me, like sitting at home having a beer with wife and brothers-in-law.

"I talked to Martha," Kate told Noah. "She's flying up tomorrow. I'll pick her up at the Hyannis airport."

"Anything new?" I asked him. "Did they do the autopsy?"

"Are you stringing for the *Globe* on this one?"

"I called them. You knew I would. I need the bread, Noah."

"I hope you didn't go into the passenger's-seat business, the possibility of there being another person involved."

"I didn't. I left it vague, for now."

"They did the autopsy. The official cause of death is by drowning."

Bascombe, still stung by the defeat, was standing on the line, throwing away with his new darts, practice, practice, practice, paying no attention to us. He wanted another game.

"They find anything else?" I asked.

"What I suspected, booze and ludes, a combination, and a sizable dose of both. Maybe as much as a pint of alcohol, probably vodka. I found a half-gallon bottle in the dorm, nearly empty, and the forensic team found an empty quart bottle of Popov on the floor of the car. The examiner says a number of Quaaludes, two or three, in her system. I'd guess Lemon 7-14. That's the most common. They go for about three bucks apiece on the street in Hyannis. Also evidence of cocaine. Not much."

"What would that combination do to a person, a healthy young adult?"

"A lude is a sedative, a downer that suppresses your involuntary systems. It reduces breathing, reduces the rate of the heartbeat."

35

I was taking notes on a napkin while Noah talked.

"Two or three of them and after fifteen minutes you're floating. Your sense of smell, your eyesight, your sense of time all become distorted. Add the booze and your physical reaction time is delayed and slowed."

"As in, you couldn't open a car door and climb out after the car went into the water," I said. "Even if you were conscious."

"Teenagers use the combination a lot when they set out to commit suicide."

"You think some sort of pact? A pact the other person backed out on?"

"I don't know what I think yet. I'm still looking into this thing."

"I can't believe it was suicide," Kate said. "Susie was too alive, too full of herself."

"Did you find anything interesting in the waitress dorm?"

"There was no sign of violence or forced entry. The door was unlocked and the place was a mess. Susan Jacobs was a slob. She'd been living out of two suitcases, sleeping on a bunk bed under a blanket, no sheets, even though they were there, stacked for the taking. Dirty clothes everywhere, dirty bathroom, you should have seen it, like a mess left behind by a spoiled child. Dede would have gone bonkers."

Dede Simmons looked like a child standing beside her husband. But at home when that little blue-jeans mother said March, everybody marched, including big Noah. She ran a spotless house with three spotless kids.

"That was Susan," Kate said. "Martha was always complaining about her sloppy ways."

"Kate, did she know anybody here besides yourself?"

"I don't think so. I told you, she just showed up. In that VW."

"I found some snapshots of her in the dorm, in her suitcase. I've had two units checking around all afternoon, at restaurants, gas stations, grocery stores, liquor stores, all over the immediate area. Three or four people recognized her face, but so far nobody remembers spotting her or the car last night."

"Maybe she never left the premises," I said.

Noah looked at me and my stack of napkins. "Incidentally, this is all off the record for the time being, Scoop."

"Oh, come on, Noah."

"You'll get it, in time, when I know more."

"I got a hunch you know more now, more than you're telling."

"Not really. When I searched the dorm I got a strong feeling that somebody had gone through her things. Also, there was a blanket and a pillow on one of the other beds, the one next to hers. I got the feeling that somebody else had been staying there with her."

4

THERE WERE THREE GARDENERS, grown men wearing green coveralls, not bare-chested kids in shorts, working on the grounds of the estate when I arrived there the next morning. If that gives you any idea.

There were dozens of other, equally big summer homes in North Walpole, but the house where Dolph Bridges was staying was both big and new, only two years old. It sat on three priceless acres of harbor-front land on the northwestern side of the Cut. Cranberry House restaurant was just across the way, maybe a hundred and fifty yards shore-to-shore at low tide. The place belonged to Bridges's campaign finance chairman, a Chicago-based investor named Charls Munro II. Why the funny spelling I didn't know.

After some initial misgivings and protests by people who thought such choice land should not be privately developed, the Munros eventually won the town's grudging approval. The house they built was both handsome and proper, big but not ostentatious, a traditional gray shingled home with sea-green shutters, white woodwork, and with a high, thick hedge surrounding it, a proper place with nothing Nantucket high-style about it. It blended well into the landscape and, except for access to a small dock, the shoreline of the property, fifteen yards back from high tide, had been left to the town for public use on the advice of some very savvy local lawyer.

Munro and his wife, Dody, had bought the land the moment it became available. Nobody knew why they chose North Walpole as their summer retreat or how they had learned the land was available, although it was said that Dody Munro had lived somewhere on the Cape briefly as a child when her father was stationed at Otis Air Force Base.

The Munros were a rather curious addition to the summer community in that they appeared to want no part of it. They knew nobody in town and had made no effort to change that. They didn't join the yacht club, although they kept a sizable boat, a big blue ketch, in Pilgrim Harbor, and they never entertained. They were not aggressive in their desire for privacy, no fences or watchdogs or anything like that. They simply kept to themselves when they were in town.

All this gossip had been provided to me by my blue-haired old sweetie at the library.

Thursday was still another clear and sunny day, the Cape at its best. If you licked your lips you tasted salt.

Kate and I had slept with the bedroom windows open the night before, that's the kind of weather it was, and I felt good that morning. I waved at the gardeners, guys I sat with from time to time at the counter at Bob's Sandwich Shop, and rang the doorbell.

A young Latin American girl wearing a black maid's uniform opened the door without speaking, and as I stepped into the foyer I saw that a big handsome man was walking forward to greet me. He was all muscle and his face was all sharp planes and angles. He was in his late thirties. He was wearing white shorts, a lime-green polo double-knit, and he had a Super Bowl ring on his left index finger. His skin was the color of wet beach sand. Thomas Duncan.

"I'm McFarland. I'm expected, I hope," I told him. We shook hands.

"Come on in. Your timing couldn't be better. From your point of view."

"I used to work in Chicago."

"Oh, I recognize your name," he said, which made me feel good. Most readers don't pay much attention to newspaper bylines.

"I feel almost like I know you, you know. You gave me a lot of Sunday afternoons of pleasure when you played for the Bears. You were the greatest."

"Those were the days."

"What's up? Why is my timing so good?"

"Gould's dropped out. We just heard about it."

"You have got to be kidding." Although he had not formally announced his candidacy, Raymond Gould was the leading conservative contender for the Republican presidential nomination, the young governor of Arizona who was as handsome as a movie star. Beautiful women in designer dresses wept and strong, otherwise restrained captains of industry stood and cheered when he spoke at fund-raisers. Ray Gould was the party's new Golden Boy.

"I kid you not," Thomas Duncan said. "He made the announcement a few minutes ago in Phoenix."

"Did he give a reason?"

"He said for personal reasons, that's all." Thomas Duncan led me through the living room—brightly decorated, sunshine yellow with lots of white and green—out to the adjacent, enclosed sun porch, which looked out on the Cut and obviously was serving as the Bridges campaign planning center. There was a Mister Coffee machine, a small refrigerator, a card table laden with yellow legal tablets, notebooks, pens and pencils. On other card tables were electric typewriters, a computer and three color-television sets. There were telephones everywhere.

I spotted Billy Nolan the moment I walked in. Black Irish Billy was overweight, always had been. He had curly black hair which was beginning to show some gray at the edges, I noticed, and deep blue eyes. An old buddy and Bridges's number one speechwriter.

He saw me, walked over, threw an arm around my shoulders and gave me a hug. "And look who the fucking cat's drug in. You doing, pal?" Dolph Bridges, I noticed, was in a far corner, talking on a phone.

"Never better, Billy." I returned the hug.

Billy Nolan had started his career as a sports and feature writer for my old paper in Chicago. We were cub reporters together. Billy could write rings around me, the son of a bitch. It came so easily for him. He sat and started moving his fingers on a typewriter keyboard and out came the words and sentences, clear, beautiful prose which (as he would say) to hear him talk you'd never know it.

From Chicago he had gone on to New York, where he became a highly paid and fairly famous magazine writer. His very first book, a funny sports novel, was made into a movie. But Billy wrote so well, his thoughts spilled over so much, that sports could not contain him. Sports was the one-way bus trip he took on the road up the hill to social commentary. Though he had been a liberal Democrat and a Jack Kennedy fanatic when we started out together, his political beliefs had changed over the years, I was not sure how or why, and now he was a conservative Republican, a convert off the street, with enough moola stashed away to be able to take time off and join the Bridges campaign. It was through him that I had arranged to write the magazine profile.

"Dolph?" he called. "Will you look what the cat's drug

in here?" Bridges had finished his phone conversation and was approaching.

I walked over and shook hands with the man. He was wearing old faded jeans, a white polo shirt and a pair of leather Docksiders, no socks. Tanned, with a full head of snow-white hair and alert chocolate-brown eyes, Dolph Bridges was a lean, vigorous-looking guy in the very prime of life. He stood out. Place him in the middle of a crowd of people and you would point to him immediately. "There. That one. That's *somebody*."

"By God, it's good to see you, McFarland. It makes it seem like old times," he said. "I'm very happy you're doing the *Times* profile."

"Thanks. So am I."

"I've told everybody we're giving you the run of the place. Blend into the wallpaper. Except we get to call it on and off the record and for background only. We got a deal?"

"We got a deal. I can live with that."

"And what's going on right now is off the record. At least for the time being. We're not quite sure what's happening here."

"Thomas told me about Gould's announcement. Amazing."

"It's either sex or it's dirty money or it's some criminal act," Billy Nolan announced.

"Well, I've got my campaign manager on the phone

over there checking it out, asking about, trying to find out exactly what it is," Bridges said to me.

"Eliot's got the best political Rolodex in the entire Republican party," Billy said. "She's the top woman in her field."

I glanced over. Eliot More sat at a card table on the far corner of the sun porch, chatting it up with somebody on a cordless phone, and, sure enough, the Rolodex was open on the table before her.

It was Deep Throat time. Given an hour and a telephone, a good national political operative can touch political bases, federal, state and local, all over the country. Inside information is their life's blood.

Dolph Bridges rubbed his eyes and took a sip from a can of Diet Coke. "It simply does not make sense."

"I never thought Governor Gould had much chance of winning the nomination," I said. "Not this time."

"You're right, he couldn't have won," Bridges said. "But he's young and dynamic and he could have won delegates in the primaries and especially at the state conventions. I mean, Ray Gould could have made a lot of noise at the national convention."

"Say he'd come out of the primaries with enough delegate strength to demand second place on a ticket with you. Would you have given it to him?" I asked.

"In a minute. He's what the party needs, smart, ambitious, a great speaker. And he says no thanks."

"I'll say it again," Billy said. "Sex, tainted bucks or a criminal act. And somebody's picked up on it."

44

"Billy, you don't know that. We had a background check done on Ray, just for our private information," Bridges said to me. "Squeaky clean, not a blip. You know his wife was killed in a plane crash a couple of years back. He's spent his time since then working hard at being governor and trying to raise two young sons by himself."

"You do know one thing," I said. *"You* didn't nail him."

"My guess is Carlson," Billy said. Frank Carlson was Senate majority leader and Dolph Bridges's most powerful rival for the nomination.

"I wouldn't put it past him," Bridges said. "The bastard."

"And also my personal guess is something in Arizona. The guy's whole life up to now has been in that one state."

"Well, we need hard information fast. A lot of potential conservative support is at stake here."

"You need his endorsement is what you need. That fucker pats you on the head and you got the vote of every right-wing nut in the country, and you know it. Except the holy rollers, of course," Billy said.

Eliot More walked over to us, phone in hand. She was about forty, I guessed, with a face that was pleasant enough, and the preppy cotton sweater and plaid skirt she was wearing, not to mention the penny loafers, made you think she must have cried real tears when Peck & Peck went out of business.

She took Dolph by the arm, ignoring my presence. "We need to talk," she said and led him away.

They stood by a window and she whispered in his ear for a few moments, until his face flushed suddenly in anger and he turned and threw his Diet Coke can across the room. "This fucking business!" he shouted. "This dirty fucking business! Wouldn't you know some low-life bastard would start trying to peddle a piece of shit like that. Five minutes after the guy announces he's not running." He walked back to where Billy and I stood and Eliot More followed him. "AIDS is what she's hearing," he said bitterly.

Billy whistled and whispered, "Jesus."

"Who fed you that crap, Eliot?"

"I got the same story from three different people, Dolph. Excellent sources," she said, with an unfriendly glance at me.

Bridges sat on a couch and covered his face with his hands. "The poor bastard. Eliot, are you absolutely certain of this?"

"I'm afraid so. They're going to call it cancer of the something. He'll be resigning as governor in about a month."

"He was a married man, for God's sake. Two little boys. The check we did on him didn't turn up anything homosexual."

"No, it didn't."

"You don't have to be queer to get it. You know that,"

Billy said. "Maybe he had a blood transfusion for something. Or got it popping some broad."

"He's never shown any interest in women since his wife died," Eliot More said. "An occasional dinner date, that's all."

"You're saying he had a latent homosexual urge all along but managed to suppress it. Is that what you're telling me?"

"Dolph, I'm telling you what I was told, that's all. I don't like this any better than you do."

Dolph Bridges shook his head in dismay.

"There was this intern in his office last fall and winter," Eliot said. "A boy from the political science department at the university. He's described as looking a lot like Brooke Shields. They were never seen together, no relationship, no gossip. The boy completed his internship and returned to school . . ."

"And now he has AIDS."

"Dolph, it's the only possible connection anybody can come up with." She shrugged her shoulders in dismay.

"Christ."

Nobody spoke for a moment. There was a feeling of emptiness in the room, emptiness and confusion, as if they had been reading a play in rehearsal and had come unexpectedly to a missing page. There usually is a missing page, or an extra one, not counted on, in most political campaigns I've observed.

"So what do we do?" Dolph asked.

"I want to suggest something," Eliot More said. "I think you ought to get your butt out to Phoenix and pay him a visit. Now, before the word gets out. No big deal, just a short visit."

"To say what to him? Sorry, but that's what you get for taking it in the butt?"

"You tell him you respect his decision and extend your very best wishes to him. Nothing more, not asking anything from him. You just happened to be out West on business and you wanted to drop by and say hello."

"I think I like it," Billy said.

Dolph sighed. "Gould's supporters will say I'm sucking up to him, trying to get him to endorse me now that he's pulled out. And I would get flak from the columnists for the same reason. Bob Novak would carve me a new asshole."

"So you take the heat," Eliot said. "A few months from now, after he resigns, when his health starts to decline, when the truth finally seeps out, and it will, then everybody will see it differently. His people will commend you for sticking by him. Some of them may even decide to support you."

"Jesus," I muttered, couldn't help it.

"And who asked you?" Eliot More said to me.

"Eliot, I said treat him like a member of the family," Dolph said.

"I don't mind telling you I was dead set against giving you the access you've been given," she said to me. "Billy

48

vouched for you and Dolph okayed it. But there are a few things you need to get through your head, my friend."

"I'm listening. Tell me."

"We are not playing games. We're out to elect this man here president of the United States. To put it another way, we're out to take over the country, which is what winning the presidency is really all about."

"I know politics is not fun and games, Miss More. I don't need a sermon from you."

"Okay, okay," Dolph said. "It's decision time."

"Give me a go on this one, Dolph," she said. "I know Gould's appointments secretary from way back. I can get you in. And Charlie Munro says his Citation's on call. He could fly in tonight." Eliot More, tense, coiled, trembling, was going snap, crackle and pop, a live power line, downed in a storm, writhing and spewing electric sparks, not the sort of person who easily takes no for an answer.

"Billy, don't we have another roundtable discussion set up for tomorrow?" Bridges asked.

"On terrorism."

"Well, you'll have to call around and cancel and reschedule. Think up some excuse."

Eliot More smiled and took a deep breath. "We'll have to be careful," she said. "Ray Gould knows he's dying. He doesn't know we know, but it won't take him long to figure it out. He's no dummy."

Thomas Duncan had been sitting in a rattan armchair all the while, observing in silence. "Do you want me to get out to Phoenix tonight and advance you?" he asked.

"God, no! That's the last thing we want," Dolph said. "We don't want to announce the visit."

"Thomas, we want the media to . . . *find out about it*," Eliot said. "Who's our state chairman in Arizona?"

"A guy named Gayle Freeman. But he lives down in Tucson."

"Maricopa County?"

"A young lawyer named Fred Dingell. He's in the state legislature. I know him. He's a stand-up type," Thomas said.

"Give him a call. Tell him Dolph's having a strictly private meeting late tomorrow morning, or early afternoon, with Gould, stopping off on his way to, what the hell, Los Angeles. Tell him Dolph plans to slip in and out, no press coverage," Eliot told him.

"But then you tell our friend Dingell *you* think it's a hell of a story that deserves press coverage," Dolph said.

"You want him to leak it," Thomas said with a smile.

"You got it."

"I assume you want this to get beyond Arizona."

"Thomas, does Tarzan swing on a vine?" Eliot asked.

I wasn't sure who was calling the shots here, but it wasn't difficult to see that Dolph and Eliot were on a media hunt together, Eliot the lioness springing at a fresh kill and Dolph an MGM aging Leo preparing to gorge himself on a political jungle wet feast.

"After Dolph sees Governor Gould, he'll walk out to

his car," Eliot said. "Where he will reluctantly spend four or five minutes talking with reporters who happen to be there. Television, too, of course. The camera crews must be alerted."

"That is the most important thing of all," Dolph Bridges said. "This is big political news and the networks have probably sent camera crews to Phoenix from L.A. to stake out the governor's office. Be very sure that our boy Dingell gets the word to them."

"And remember, Thomas, this is *your* idea," Eliot said. "Tell Dingell Dolph would murder you if he found out you were leaking advance word about this visit. We want the reporters to *write* that, Thomas. You got it?"

"I tell the truth. I guess this's not lying. Close, though."

Dolph and Eliot stood thinking, breathing deeply. "It'll work," she said. "It's going to work." She lit a cigarette and shivered, as if with fever.

"How do you like being on the inside so far, Mac?" Dolph asked. "This is all very much off the record, to put it mildly."

"I know it's a rough business, running for president. Two or three books are written saying that after every election."

"This is *not* dirty pool, damn it," Eliot said angrily. "Hardball politics, rough politics, grown-up stuff, you bet. But not dirty. That's exactly what gave me doubts about bringing you into this, McFarland."

"So far you have my word it's all off the record. When I decide to change the rules, all of you will know."

"Mac knows politics," Billy said. "Also, his word is good as gold."

"You want to fly out to Phoenix with us tomorrow?" Dolph asked me. "The flight out and back might give us a chance to talk."

"Sure, if I don't crowd you."

"I'm going to raise Fred Dingell on the phone," Thomas said. "You know, I sure feel sorry for that poor governor in Arizona. Because he's doomed."

"Me, too," Eliot said. "It's too bad. He had a very bright future ahead of him in national politics, no doubt about that."

"Yeah, he might have been one of your big accounts a few years from now," Billy said. "Think of the money you'll lose."

"How would you like to kiss my ass?"

"Come on. We all feel sorry for Governor Gould," Dolph Bridges said. He looked at his watch. "Now, I've got a telephone talk-show interview with some station in Iowa in fifteen minutes. Then I'm going to take a nap. What a day."

5

I HAD LUNCH WITH BILLY NOLAN and Thomas Duncan
on the patio, which overlooked the tennis court,
the swimming pool and the boat dock. Thomas and I
were served chilled melon soup, lobster salad and an
excellent white wine. Billy had a six-pack of Bud and a
rare hamburger. "Seafood gives me gas," he explained
to me.

It was one-thirty in the afternoon and Dolph was taking his nap. "One hour every day after lunch," Billy said.
"I think he read somewhere that's what Jack Kennedy
done."

Before that he sat on the sun porch and did the talk
show with a little radio station in Ottumwa, Iowa. The
Iowa precinct caucuses, held in February every presidential election year, is the nation's first test of a candidate's
strength and popularity with voters, a media event that
draws hundreds of reporters. That caucus night was still
a full twenty months away, but Dolph was already work-

ing the territory, and he was not alone. So were all the other potential candidates.

"Where did Eliot get off to?" I asked.

"Probably in the library reading fucking Machiavelli," Billy said. "Checking it out to see if she's missed anything."

"What are these roundtable discussions Dolph was talking about? Anything I'd be interested in?"

"Yeah, probably. Bullshit but good copy. See, one of the big things we're doing right now is working on issues, every issue you can think of, deciding exactly where Dolph stands and putting it down on paper."

"Doesn't he already know where he stands?"

"They like to be consulted," Thomas said. "Only natural."

"Hell, I know what you're doing. You're blowing up the balloon, making sure there are no holes in it before you send it up. You don't want to be caught on the wrong side of any issue."

"See, these one-issue bastards drive you crazy these days," Billy said. "You disagree with them on their pet topic, they're against you, period. So you got to do the wiggle, stay far enough to the right to win the nomination, then wiggle to the middle to win the support of the mainstream Republican voters, then in the general election wiggle some more so you won't scare off the independents and the Democrat crossovers."

"Who are you calling in? Businessmen? Right-wing nuts?"

"Both. Look, we let them have their say, string a mike around their necks and tell them we're putting them on tape because we don't want to forget one word of their advice."

"And hope you give the impression that you're keeping an open mind."

"You know anybody ever ran for president and *won* who didn't do the same thing?"

"No."

"Besides, they're not our biggest problem. It's protecting Dolph from the press," Billy said. "Up all political reporters."

"I'm not out to get him, Billy. Hell, I like the guy."

"I know that. Otherwise you wouldn't be here. But remember, this is an election with no incumbent. So what's the dream of every reporter covering it? To knock off one of the candidates, that's what."

"That's paranoid."

"I been there, remember? I been in that pack. Old guys trying to hang in there, kids trying to make their mark. They're all headhunters who'll pounce on any little mistake and magnify it."

I knew what he was talking about. George Romney said he had been brainwashed on Vietnam. So long, George. Ed Muskie threw a temper tantrum on a flatbed truck outside the Manchester *Union-Leader* building in New Hampshire. Get out of here, Eddie.

"You run an efficient campaign, they write that you're a ruthless fucking machine. First little thing goes wrong

and they write that your campaign's a shambles."
Thomas shook his head.

"Worse than that. Try to keep a little distance between reporters and your candidate, give your guy a little breathing room, Christ' sake, they write about how isolated and out of touch with reality he is. He has a drink on the plane while he chats you guys up, rumor is he's a drunk. He kisses one of his secretaries on her cheek because it's her birthday and the staff got her a cake, rumor is he's banging her at every overnight." Billy snorted.

"Ambush journalism," I said.

"Believe it. Nothing's off the record no more with these guys. See, from here on, until primary season starts, the press don't have all that much to write about, so you got to guard against the least mistake or it gets blown up."

"I advance every public appearance Dolph makes," Thomas said. "I don't want no slip-ups. No half-empty halls. No lunatics sharing the head table. No picket lines to cross."

"If Dolph wins, what would you like to get out of it, Thomas?" I asked.

"He plays his cards right, he might get to be ambassador to one of them African countries nobody can find even on the latest *National Geographic* map," Billy said. He had finished his sixth beer, I noticed.

"My ass is a juicy peach. Bite it, Billy."

Billy waved his empty beer can at a young uniformed maid who was standing just inside the sun porch. "Hey, Maria. *Tres más, por favor*."

"What are you, on a diet or something?" I asked.

"Nine beers and a nap until dinner. Every day," Thomas said.

"How about the National Council on the Handicapped? That's right down your alley," Billy said to him.

"I didn't do it, Billy. It was not my idea. A very large defensive end named Midnight Pearson did it."

"This gimp here?" Billy said, waving the beer can at Thomas. "Just the best natural athlete in the history of the world is all. Including all them Olympic Greeks."

"I've seen Thomas play football many times. Thomas, I saw you beat the Steelers all by yourself one Sunday in Chicago. Four touchdowns."

"When he was playing for the Bears and I was writing free-lance pieces for *Sports Illustrated,* I was practically his personal publicity agent. And you can't deny that, Thomas."

"Thomas was your ticket to the big time, too, Billy. And you can't deny *that.*"

"There never was another man born who could run with a football like this beautiful blackbird here. Brown, Sayers, Payton, better than any of them. It was a privilege to watch him play the game. Until he broke his fucking leg. I heard the damn thing snap all the way up in the

57

press box, over the noise." Billy clapped his hands together. "Like a rifle shot."

"I can still hear it," Thomas said.

"I bet you can. Because you never were worth a damn after that. Only two and a half pro seasons."

"Billy, anybody ever tell you you got a big mouth?" I asked.

"Going on nine beers. Don't pay any attention to him, Mac," Thomas said. "I'm doing okay."

"Except you want respect again. Which is why you're working for Dolph. Not to mention the fact that you need the money," Billy said.

"I don't deny that. Mac, I'm thirty-seven now and I would like to hold some position of responsibility in the federal government, if Dolph wins."

"I hope it comes true for you," I told him.

A woman had walked out on the tennis court, a tanned woman dressed in a white one-piece tennis outfit. She wore her ash-blond hair pulled back in a bun. With her was a young man who was carrying a big canvas bag filled with yellow tennis balls. She waved at us and both Billy and Thomas waved back.

"The new wife?" I asked.

"If you call married for five years new," Billy said.

"I knew Dolph's first wife slightly, from his first campaign for Congress."

"Patricia. She died ten years ago."

"No kids, right?"

"It's my understanding Patricia couldn't."

"No kids with this new one either, not yet and probably never," Thomas said.

"I know her name's Helen. I read it in the library clips."

"Family name, her grandmother's name," Billy said. "That one down there swinging that racket is one of your genuine, old-line Washington society princesses, cliff dwellers or cave dwellers, or whatever it is they call them down there. And not a cent to her name. They live off Dolph's income."

"Which obviously is enough to afford tennis lessons."

Helen Bridges and the young man were rallying. He was a machine and she was not bad, either. A tall, raw-boned woman with broad shoulders, she had good, fluid strokes, she moved across the court quickly and easily, and she hit the ball hard.

"Dolph's not paying. Munro is," Billy said.

"Charls Munro is a generous man."

"It was all set up for us, Mac. Hot and cold running everything, cars, cooks, maids, tennis pro on call, like a hotel. All we thought we were getting was a quiet place to get our act together."

"Mrs. Bridges seems to take right to it."

"See, it was like this for her when she was a kid growing up in Middleburg, Virginia."

"What happened? Something bad, obviously."

"Helen's blueblood daddy spent all the money, as I

understand it, without it ever entering his mind that one day the bucks would give out, which they did. I guess he thought he was a poet. When all the money was gone he blew his brains out."

"She'd been married before."

"To a gentleman bum, when she was a kid. All he did was ride horses. I'm told he could jump a horse over the moon. Helen there had to sell off land around the family farm piece by piece to developers to support them. He broke his neck on one of those jumps. There weren't a lot of tears."

On the court, Helen Bridges took the young pro's best service and sent it back down the line, low and so hard that it made the tape go pop when the ball hit it. "Lady, you don't need me," the pro shouted.

"How old is she?"

"Forty-two."

"She doesn't look it."

"It's full-time maintenance with Helen. She's a health nut. Vegetarian, except for a little broiled fish now and then. She don't smoke, she don't drink, not even wine. She runs on the beach here every morning, swims every afternoon, and hits the sack early. Christ' sake, who wouldn't be healthy? Even you and me, McFarland."

"What sort of a person? She sounds like a female jock."

"No bitch, if that's what you're saying. She's just one of those people who've got to huff and puff, exercise all the time."

"I'm going to need to talk to her, spend some time with her."

"When the time is right." He popped his ninth beer. "We need the *Times* profile. You know that. It's their way of declaring somebody a legitimate candidate. Frankly, what I don't understand, and no hard feelings, is why they picked you to do it. Usually, when they go free lance they get some alumnus from the paper, Dick Reeves, Tony Lucas, guys they know and trust."

"I think I sold them because I know Dolph from way back."

"I heard you quit the paper back in Chicago."

"Fired, Billy. There's no polite way to put it. I didn't fit into their new game plan."

"See, this is what I heard, that you were canned. So how'd you end up here?"

"By accident. Also my wife screwed me over. You never knew her. I ran away, truth be known."

"Some beautician, I heard."

"A dental technician. Give me a little credit, will you?"

"And now you're up here in the boonies, free-lancing. Tough way to make a living, and I ought to know."

"I'm getting by. It doesn't take so much up here."

I thought about my bank balance, which was like a gas gauge showing a tad above empty when you're driving late at night on a long and empty road. In the rain. Getting by. Close to being broke I was.

I looked across the Cut at Cranberry House. I could see the broken railing where Susan Jacobs's VW had

61

crashed through and plunged into the water. There were three or four cars and a couple of delivery trucks in the parking lot. This was Thursday and the restaurant would be opening for the season on Saturday. Nat Loory's staff was there, cleaning, storing, readying for it.

"I string for the Boston *Globe*," I told Billy. "The regional editor there's a friend of mine. He throws work my way."

"What work? Nothing ever happens here except the tide changes."

"We had a drowning this week. At that restaurant right over there. See the broken railing? A car went through it and a young woman was drowned."

"So what did you file, two, three hundred words?"

"You got it. But things will pick up with the summer season. Thousands of people from Boston come out here then and the *Globe* prints lots of Cape stories."

While Billy and I were talking, Helen Bridges had finished her tennis session, dismissed the young pro, and had gone inside a cabana that sat between the court and the pool. Now she walked out of the cabana, wearing a skintight black tank suit and carrying a towel, flippers and a face mask in her hands.

"Look at that body, will you?" Billy said. "Like a temple. In perfect, mint condition."

Helen walked past the pool out to the boat dock, donned the mask and flippers, and jumped in.

"She hates the pool, won't go near it," Billy said. "She

hates the chlorine, or whatever they treat the water with these days. She loves salt water and she's a strong swimmer. She'll do three or four miles before she comes in."

Helen Bridges was doing a steady, measured crawl, strong and sure. The three of us sat and watched her in admiration. In only a few minutes she made it through the Cut and her head was a tiny dot bobbing in the choppy blue-gray water of Nantucket Sound.

"Every afternoon she swims like this?"

"We been up here a week now and every day so far she has," Thomas said. "Too cold for me but she seems to like it."

"Hers truly is some body," I said. "That's a good-looking woman."

"Dolph makes it, Helen Bridges will be the next Jackie Kennedy. Queen of America," Billy said. "Wait and see."

6

WHEN I GOT HOME that afternoon, Kate was serving tea to her college roommate, Martha Jacobs, and she was making an occasion of it. There were small crustless cucumber and watercress sandwiches, she was using the fancy china, and the tea was being poured from a huge, ornate silver service I had never seen before.

Kate introduced us, describing me as "my friend, Mac McFarland," and Martha Jacobs looked at me with cold slate-gray eyes that clearly said *I know you're living with her*. "Noah should be here any minute," Kate said, sounding a little anxious. "Want some tea?"

"Sure." I sat on the sofa and helped myself to a cucumber sandwich while Kate poured for me. I told Martha Jacobs it was nice to meet her and I was sorry about her sister's death.

"I have a court date tomorrow morning I simply cannot miss," she said. "I have a six o'clock flight out of Hyannis that connects me with a seven-forty Delta back to Washington."

"That doesn't give you much time to talk with the police chief."

"Then he'd better get his ass in gear is all I can say. Kate, I cannot contend with this crap." Martha Jacobs looked at her watch and tapped her foot.

Kate poured more tea for her and glanced at me helplessly.

"I mean, I'm more than willing to retain a local lawyer to take care of all the details," Martha said. "Anybody you suggest. I want it off my hands."

"I'm sure Noah Simmons will be able to advise you on that," I said.

She looked at her watch again.

Past thin, she was skinny, with olive complexion and an attractive face, which she obviously didn't find very challenging because she wore no makeup, no lipstick, nothing. Her hair was flat and lifeless. Her light gray business suit was obviously expensive, but it was at least one size too large for her. It looked like something she had bought at a Junior League thrift shop on an afternoon when she had left her glasses at home. Beside the chair she sat in was a leather briefcase, which I just knew was packed with important legal papers to be read and marked up on the trip back to Washington.

A piece of work, Martha Jacobs was, a busy woman, smart, abrupt and impatient, mid-career, somebody who didn't want to be bothered. That was the impression she made. I couldn't imagine Kate sharing the same college room with her for four years.

"What arrangements are you making for your sister's burial?" I asked. "I used to live in Chicago. I know the town pretty well. Anything I can do to help?"

If looks could kill, the look Kate gave me would have made me go paws up. "I'm working with Martha on that," she said firmly.

"Cremation," Martha said. "Simple and convenient." That was when Noah rang the doorbell, thank God because I would have said something to her. Such as, Glad you're not my sister.

"I really don't have much time for you, I'm afraid," was the greeting Noah got when he entered the room.

He gave her a sharp look. "It shouldn't take very long, Miss Jacobs. I'm sorry if you've been kept waiting. I was out of my office on business." Out of touch, in his wet suit, swimming in the sound, was my guess, judging from his wet hair.

"Let's begin, shall we?" she said. "Any details I can't provide now or questions that might occur to you later we can cover with a deposition, I'm sure."

"I've got this tape recorder here. Do you mind if I turn it on? That way I don't have to take notes." He sat down on the couch beside her.

"That's quite all right. I'm an attorney, remember?"

"Of course. Now, regarding your sister's death . . ."

"An accident, I'm given to believe."

"I'm not sure yet what happened."

"Not suicide."

66

"We found her body in the passenger's seat. Alone. Belted."

The young woman's face flushed. Martha Jacobs didn't like to be surprised. "Chief Simmons, are you suggesting the possibility of violent death? Murder?"

"I am suggesting that you allow me to begin my questioning."

She held her right hand out, palm up, the way opposing lawyers in conference do it to signal *Go ahead, you first*.

"To your knowledge, did your sister use drugs?"

"You must understand that Susan was not actually my sister. She was adopted as an infant by my parents when I was four years old."

"So Kate has informed me."

"She was never an addict. I think I can say that. But, yes, when she was a teenager, in high school, she smoked a lot of pot. She was suspended once when she showed up in class stoned. You can imagine how disturbed my parents were."

"Cocaine?"

"When she was older. When it was available."

"Heroin?"

"Never. She told me she was afraid of it."

"You're sure of all this? It's my understanding from Kate that the two of you were not very close."

"That's correct. But we did grow up together, after all. Susie, Susan, confided in me, sometimes, when she felt she had the need."

67

"Quaaludes?"

"I suppose so. If something was available, Susan would try just about anything once. What is this, anyway? I don't quite understand where this line of questioning is supposed to be leading us."

"Your sister had taken two or three Quaaludes the night she died. Also some cocaine, probably earlier in the evening."

"That's a lot. Almost an overdose of Quaaludes, I think."

"Yes, it is. Was she a heavy drinker, Miss Jacobs? She had also consumed about a pint of alcohol that night. Probably vodka. I found a bottle at the place where she was staying. And we found another empty vodka bottle on the floor, in the backseat of her car."

"She wasn't an alcoholic. But, yes, she drank. Again, it depended on the situation, who she was with, what was available, what was going on. Susan was uninhibited. If everybody else was getting loaded, then she would get loaded. She lived for the moment, you might say."

"Was she in the habit of drinking alone, do you know?"

"Sometimes. She used to raid the bar at home when she was a teenager. One night, I was in college then, my parents came home from the opera and found her passed out on the living room floor."

"So it's not inconceivable that she would buy herself a bottle of vodka and keep it in her room here? And drink it alone?"

"No. I've told you, Susan acted on impulse. All her life. You never knew what she was going to do next until she did it. It used to drive my parents crazy."

"Do you have any idea why she left her job in Washington and came here? Did she discuss the move with you?"

Martha shrugged her shoulders. "I have no idea. I didn't even know she *had* left Washington until Kate called and told me she was dead. Weeks, sometimes months, would go by with no communication between us, Chief Simmons."

"Was she in any trouble that you were aware of? Personal problems? Debts?"

"Was she pregnant?" Martha asked suddenly. "Did the autopsy show that?"

"No, she wasn't. Why do you ask?"

"Because it wouldn't be the first time. It happened twice before, with yours truly footing the bill both times."

"But she hadn't come to you recently, asking for your help, for any reason?"

"No, she hadn't. I put my foot down after I bought her the car and helped her get her place furnished. Enough's enough."

"Let me just say, I think I understand how frustrating it must have been for someone like you to have to deal with someone like her. I'm trying to get a fix on a person I didn't know, so bear with me, please."

"I quite understand." Martha turned to Kate. "The

69

tea's terrific, but could I have a little vodka? Neat. With maybe a small glass of grapefruit juice on the side?"

Noah turned off his tape recorder. "Time out."

I got up and made the drinks, vodka for Martha Jacobs, white wine for Kate, and a couple of knocks of George Dickel sour mash on the rocks for Noah and me.

"Nice room," Martha said, taking a look around while she tossed down the vodka. "Worth a fortune, too, and I should know. I'm in the process of moving and I've hired a decorator. I have no sense for that sort of thing myself, as you well know, Katie." She finished her drink, and I hurried back to the bar to pour her another one, a semitriple this time, after I saw Noah's slight nod of assent.

Martha was correct, it was a very tony room in which we were sitting. A few years before her death, Jane Drexel, the old lady who had owned the house and willed it to Kate, decided it was time to redecorate and hired a famous and expensive New York firm to do it, with in-structions to spare no reasonable expense. A decorator's dream, I suppose, like an editor telling a reporter, "Fly to London. First class, of course. Stay at Claridge's. Spare no expense. File me a piece a week, seven hundred words for the Sunday edition, on the English mood."

I'm a K Mart man myself, whose taste runs to modern Danish, but Kate had given me a crash course in grand design. The room had lemon-yellow Stark carpeting with green vines woven around its borders, a pair of overstuffed sofas and armchairs upholstered with Brunschwig et Fils fabric, an eighteenth-century English secretary and a satinwood Chippendale chest-on-chest. Two J.M.W. Turner watercolor landscapes were hanging on the walls. I was slowly getting used to it.

Noah finished his drink. "I know you're anxious to make your flight." He pushed the Record button on his Sony. "Now, as I understand it from Kate, you helped your sister get located in Washington."

"That's correct. Almost two years ago. I was an associate then at Holland Wheatley and up to my ears in work."

"Martha's just been made a full partner," Kate said proudly.

Martha smiled in recognition of the tribute, then went on with her story. "I hadn't heard from her in months and months. She had been living with some married guy somewhere in northern California, spending the money that was left to her in my parents' will."

"And when it was gone, she turned to you?"

"As usual."

"And as usual, you came through."

Martha shrugged her shoulders. "I sent her airfare. She was broke, and she and the guy had split up. I got her into a little efficiency apartment on Capitol Hill. She damn well wasn't about to move in with me. And I made the down payment on the car. You've got to have a car to live in Washington. I co-signed for it."

"Where did you find her work?"

Martha smiled, for the first time, remembering the moment. "The job found her, really. She'd been in town for only a week or so. The two of us went out to Wolf Trap to see *The Marriage of Figaro*. That's one thing Susan did get from my parents, an appreciation of opera, from being carted to productions in Chicago and listening to records constantly at home. The Mozart was sold out that night, so we got tickets to sit on the lawn, more fun anyway. We took a blanket and a bottle of wine, and we happened to find a place on the grass next to a guy I used to go out with, never anything serious between us, understand. We talked and Gary said he had just been promoted to staff director on the Bridges Foreign Relations Subcommittee and he said he had an opening for a clerk-typist. Susan went to work a week later. Blind luck. She was always lucky, that one. Well, you know, I mean until now."

Nobody spoke for a moment, a moment when Susan Jacobs was very much with us. Then Martha cleared her throat and the well-trained lawyer that she was took over.

"How was the car discovered?" she asked quietly. "Who found my sister?"

"I did," I said. "I pulled her out of the car and attempted to revive her."

"Chief, her body was found in the front passenger's seat?"

"That is correct."

"Mr. McFarland, you found her. How did she *look*?"

I glanced at Noah and his eyes told me *Tell her*. "Eyes closed, mouth open," I said. "Belted in the seat. She looked to me like she had passed out, to tell the truth."

"I presume there was an autopsy," Martha Jacobs said to Noah. "You mentioned the alcohol and the drugs found in her body. Did you discover any evidence of physical violence? Bruises? Wounds? Sexual abuse?"

"No. We didn't."

"Whoever was driving got out and left her to drown. That's what happened, isn't it?"

"That's the way it looks to me, Miss Jacobs," Noah said.

"Some bastard, whoever ran the car into the water, got out and swam away and left Susan to drown. That's what happened."

"As I said, that would seem to be the case," Noah said. "We are investigating all this very thoroughly, I assure you. Right now, to be honest, we have no suspects. That's where I was hoping you could help us."

"I doubt it. It's manslaughter, you know. At least."

"I know. Could we go on? I don't have much more."

She held her palm out again. Proceed.

"She got a job. She then spent the next two years or so working in Washington, correct? Who were her friends? How'd she spend her free time?"

"She had her life and I had mine. Understand, I was working my ass off, and I'd made friends of my own. You

73

know how it is. But she'd call from time to time, or I'd call her, and now and then we'd get together for lunch, usually on Saturdays. But it would take a team of experts a year or so to compile an accurate record of Susan's two years in Washington."

"She got around, you mean?"

"She and that town were made for each other. She truly found her home there."

"Lots of men, boyfriends? She was certainly attractive."

"Of all descriptions. Rich divorced men who took her to the charity balls, one night even to the Waltz, which is *very* social. Divorced, single, separated, *married*, it never mattered to Susan. Age, color, social status, that didn't matter either. She was a free spirit."

"Was she a nymphomaniac?"

"I wouldn't go that far. No, a born hell raiser, that's all."

"Was there ever anybody special she mentioned to you? Was she ever in love?"

"Look, Chief Simmons, my sister was an inconstant person with an emotional attention span of perhaps five minutes, no longer. Except for opera she had no intellectual or cultural interests, none. Rock music, men, parties, clubs, good times, that's what she was into. But understand, bright enough in her own way, no dummy."

"Did she ever mention names in your talks?"

"No. Probably because she had trouble keeping them

all straight. It was this guy I met. Or this cool brown stud. Or this man who's old enough to be our father. Or this really cute guy."

"Never any specific details?"

"Oh, a few. She showed up at Clyde's one day for lunch sporting a new ruby ring and I asked her about it. She told me there was this old—actually, she said ancient—Southern senator who liked to come to her apartment and hold her hand and talk. I don't know. Once she told me she'd spent a night in the Lincoln bedroom at the White House when the president and his family were out of town. I didn't know whether to believe her or not. She was not a congenital liar, by the way. I know one guy she really seemed to like was a redneck marine corporal stationed at Quantico. She met him in a rock bar in Georgetown. He took her to honky-tonks out in northern Virginia, and my guess is, made her feel right at home, hillbilly at heart that she was. Some lobbyist who took her to Atlantic City two or three weekends and let her play blackjack to her heart's content. And for a while there was some rich man who really spent money on her."

"No hint of identification?"

"No. But for a couple of months there, it was like *Come on down*! Matched Gucci luggage, designer dresses."

"Was there anybody at work? Did she have a fling with anybody at the Capitol she told you about? In her office?"

Martha thought about it. "No, no office romance that she ever mentioned. But that doesn't mean there couldn't have been one."

"She was on the town, then, young, pretty and, from your description, available."

"Susan led men on. She had a bad habit of making promises she never meant to keep, of saying things she didn't mean. I've told you that. Look, I don't have that much time left."

"A bad seed?" Noah asked quietly.

"She wasn't a monster, if that's what you're implying, not evil. She never hurt anybody. She wasn't spiteful or petty or mean, if that's what you mean. What are you? A would-be lawyer?"

"Was she ever in love? Wild over a man?"

"Crushes. Infatuations. I don't think she ever loved anybody."

"I think you're wrong. I think she loved you, Martha. You were her anchor. Her sister. I also think you loved her far more than you like to admit."

Martha looked down at her lap. "Shit," she said in a whisper. Kate rose quickly from her chair, walked over and stood behind her, placed her hands on Martha's shoulders, and gazed solemnly at Noah and me. This interview was over.

"I am sorry, but I've got a plane I must catch," Martha said, not looking up.

"I won't keep you any longer and I thank you for your time," Noah said. "I'll keep you informed."

"Shit," Martha said again.

"It's okay, Martha," Kate said.

"I mean, I remember the day they brought her home, Kate. I wasn't jealous, damn it. I held her, just a baby, only a few weeks old. I remember. I wanted a baby sister. I was *glad* to see her arrive. I was four years old, Kate."

"I can arrange a ride for you to the Hyannis airport, if you'd like," Noah said.

"I'm going to drive her," Kate said.

"Shit." Martha shook her head in grief and desperation. "I put up with a lot from her. All my life. I really tried. You know how hard I tried, Kate."

Kate motioned with her head for Noah and me to get the hell out, then knelt beside Martha and took both her hands into her own. "I know you did. I know how much you loved her."

Martha closed her eyes. "Shit, shit, *shit*. I've got a big case in court tomorrow morning. I mean, I tried to be close to her. All our lives. I helped her again and again when she got in trouble and came to me. I stood by her. Didn't I?"

"Of course you did," Kate said. "Martha, listen to me. You don't want to have her body cremated. You know you don't. Have her body sent home to Illinois and buried beside your parents. That's what they'd want and you, too. I'll take care of all the details here and I'll go out with you. I promise."

"I guess. Okay. Shit." Martha put her face in her hands and burst into tears. Kate threw her arms around her and held on tightly. "Oh, God, my little Susie," Martha moaned. "You know how I loved her. You know that, Kate."

Noah and I left them, walked out to the kitchen, where I poured a little more George Dickel for both of us.

"First of all, don't write it, McFarland," Noah said. "Wait for a go-ahead from me. Otherwise you'll screw up my investigation."

"Okay. I'll sit on it. But you heard her."

"Hell, yes, I heard her. I'm not deaf, Mac."

"Susan Jacobs worked on the staff of a Senate subcommittee that was chaired by Dolph Bridges."

"It could be, it doesn't amount to a thing, coincidence."

"But it's the first connection you've come across. And it suggests a lot of questions."

"I know."

"Did she follow him up here? Or one of the others working for him? Did they know she was in town?"

"You know what I feel like? Like I've just opened the locker. And there's the suitcase inside. And inside the suitcase something's ticking."

"Noah, I'm flying out to Phoenix with him tomorrow morning."

7

I DROVE OVER TO SIMMONS'S Fish Market (another of Noah's many cousins, of course) and bought two swordfish steaks for supper. Caught that morning, the clerk assured me, and I believed him. I took the fish home, opened myself a bottle of beer and sat on the patio, drinking and waiting for Kate to return from the Hyannis airport.

Maybe I should set the table, I thought. Put out some candles, toss a small green salad, maybe crack some eggs and whip up a light and tasty meringue for dessert afterwards. Wimp. For the first time in my adult life I was dependent on a woman for financial support, for food and shelter, and I didn't like it.

Kate ran the North Walpole Preservation Society with the help of a pregnant secretary named Bridget. It was a fifty-million-dollar trust that had been created to preserve and enhance the quality of life in this little Cape Cod town. That meant Kate could use the annual interest almost any way she saw fit and receive an annual salary, the amount specified by the terms of the trust, of one hundred thousand dollars for doing it. And the house came with the job.

Why such a huge salary? Because Kate most likely was the illegitimate and unacknowledged daughter of Jane Drexel, the rich old widow who had financed her higher education (Kate was a Harvard Ph.D.), and so the old lady had generously provided for her pet and protégée in her will. A widowed nurse who had previously been a Drexel employee had raised Kate as her own child. I knew all this. Kate didn't, but she accepted the big paycheck and lived in the old lady's mansion as if she knew it was her heritage. It made you wonder.

Noah Simmons and Bascombe Midgeley, my darts partner, were the other two active trustees, but they had their own jobs to occupy them, and a fourth trustee, a retired private-school teacher who probably was Kate's real father, was confined to a nursing home with Alzheimer's disease. So all the requests for grants and awards from the Preservation Society came to Kate, along with the paperwork and the finances. She ran the shop and called the shots.

With all that money under her control, Katherine Mary O'Doul Bingham had quickly become one of North Walpole's most powerful citizens, a role she was accepting without hesitation, indeed with considerable relish. The exercise of authority came naturally to her. If Kate had become a nun, she would have ended up, no doubt, as the first female president of Notre Dame.

She was an Irish Catholic woman of firm principle, strong will and unpredictable temperament and, until I came along, a thirty-one-year-old virgin widow whose brand-new husband had died on the afternoon of their wedding day in a freak private aircraft accident.

Now we were lovers, Katie and I, living together openly and without apology that springtime, the talk of the town, you may be sure, and the subject of endless speculation because the good people of North Walpole weren't entirely sure she and I hadn't slipped off somewhere and secretly tied the knot. The town's four thousand permanent residents, those who endured the long, gloomy winters, knew Kate's story right down to the last public detail. Every small town I've ever known has its ongoing soap opera, and in North Walpole's, hers was a major role.

Town talk had me down as a bachelor, a globe-trotting news reporter whose career had taken him from continent to continent and from woman to woman until Kate lassoed me. The awful truth was that I was trying to divorce an unfaithful wife who was giving me trouble. I had signed a divorce agreement and she had taken all my money, such as it was, including my severance pay from my old newspaper, but so far she had not actually filed for the divorce. Her name was Earline, and you can take it from there if you have any imagination at all.

An old friend back in Chicago, an aging copy editor who drank and smoked too much and who was one of the few people I ever completely trusted, forwarded my mail to me, and Kate let it ride without comment until the third letter from Earline arrived, blood-red envelope, white ink, addressed to Mr. "Horace" McFarland, her idea of a joke between us.

"She wants you back, doesn't she?" she said. "Her kind always does. And I think maybe you ought to think about it, my friend."

"Nobody told you it was going to be easy."

"If she wants to start over, if she's genuinely contrite, she deserves the chance, you know." Kate's eyes blazing.

"A fairly nice guy. Does the best he can. Not an enemy in the world that I know of. Don't I deserve one little fuckup, Kate?"

"No!"

"If you kick me out, I'll never go back to her. You know that. I'll go away, but I'll never go back to her. Do you want to read her letter?" I offered it to her.

"No! I don't even want to touch the damn letter. I want you to pack your things and leave, get out of here."

I got up. "It'll take me half an hour."

"How dare you be in communication with her?"

"Kate, I don't communicate with her. She communicated with me."

"Well. What does she want? I know what she wants. She wants you back."

"She had an affair with the dentist she worked for. I told you that. That didn't work out. She found another guy, a guy who does play-by-play Chicago professional basketball, and that didn't work out either. Now she's saying she has a persistent back problem that may require long-range medical attention, and that's why she hasn't filed for the divorce. I'm telling you, the fucking woman is as healthy as a Clydesdale horse."

"Then why don't you file?"

"If for some reason she contested, the thing could drag on for years, that's why. Kate, I know her—"

"I am sure you do."

"Give her a little time, she'll latch on to somebody. She's good at that. She can get no more out of me, I promise you that."

Kate took off her glasses and rubbed the bridge of her nose. "McFarland, tell me one thing. When you were in flight, coming through Providence in that wreck you call a car, why didn't you keep on going to Boston? Why did you turn right to Cape Cod?"

"I was looking for you, Kate."

"And you found me." She put her arms around my neck. "Do something, please. I'm okay for now. But I can't have her on my back forever, okay?"

And that's how we stood. Kate and I did nothing to discourage the rumor that we were secretly married; we quietly promoted it, in fact, whenever possible, attended parties together, made no bones about it. As far as she was concerned, we were living in sin, but she was going along with it, at least for the time being.

Our union had even been blessed, and it only cost two hundred thousand dollars.

In March we said to hell with trying to keep up appearances, moved our personal effects into Jane Drexel's mansion, and set up housekeeping. On our first evening there I popped for a bottle of fairly good champagne and she and I were sitting on the couch in the library, enjoying the wine and a fire, when the doorbell rang.

It was Father Terrance Riley, the pastor of Saint John's R.C. Church and good and drunk he was. Riley was a southie from Boston with brains to spare, a big guy, and he was wearing his favorite off-duty gear, jeans, sneakers and a Holy Cross sweatshirt, no coat, no hat, despite the fact that a thick, wet snow was falling outside. That happens on the Cape in the early spring; snow, like a well-known and trusted bum, keeps knocking occasionally on the door. Riley stood there in the doorway after I answered the bell, swaying, trying his best to keep his balance, his head and shoulders covered with the snow, his face beet-red. He was about my age, my size, too, and I considered him a friend, almost as close as Noah, in his own way. He burped, then smiled in apology.

"Oh, my," I said. "I know we're not living in the Middle Ages anymore and I believe in letting you guys climb over the wall and go out for a beer now and then. But you're supposed to be back by sundown. You know that."

"I've come to have a word with Kate." He stumbled past me into the library and came to a halt at the couch, grasped an arm of it to steady himself. "I am quite drunk," he announced. "In fact, I have never been quite so drunk in my entire life."

Kate was not angry, but not amused either. "Obviously you have received our letter," she said, tough and all business.

"Oh, my. Yes, I did. My goodness, yes, I did, I did, Kate. Yes, I did receive that letter." The priest cupped her face in his hands, kissed her on the forehead and then on both cheeks. "Indeed I did." Kate blushed, too old to be kissed by a priest. Especially a drunk one.

"Where have you been, at the Binnacle?" I asked.

"Oh, my. I spent the whole day at Cape Cod hospital, old men, old women, listening to confessions, a load of laughs, let me tell you. So I didn't get to the mail until I returned to the rectory and changed my clothes. There it was, and I've been drinking ever since. And I'm going to keep on drinking all night long and well into tomorrow."

"Keep your end of the bargain, that's all."

"You've saved us, Kate. You know that."

"I'm a friend, remember?" I said. "Why not let me in on it?"

"Kate here—"

"The trust, Father Riley," she said sharply, correcting him.

"*Somebody* has given Saint John's two hundred thousand dollars for school repair."

"Because the place is a wreck, that's why," Kate said. "And you have a lot of parents here in town who still insist that their children go there."

"The school is an absolute shambles. I was seriously considering closing the doors next fall. That or doubling tuition, which would have amounted to the same thing. Kate, I read your letter carefully. If you want the gift to be announced as one from an anonymous donor, no credit to the trust, so be it."

"We can't be that generous to everybody. Better that it's kept quiet. Besides, I don't want the word getting out that the first thing Kate O'Doul did with all that trust money was give her old church a big pot filled with it. You can understand that. The board made the grant because of an obvious social and civic need."

"I'll take it any way I can get it," Terrance Riley said. "I'll say Yoko Ono gave it to us if you like."

"One more drink and you'll crawl home," I said. "Want one?"

"Anything brown you have. No ice." He fell into a chair next to Kate. Terry Riley was not a drinking man, just wine and beer, but that evening, with the burden of his parish school's debt and state of ill repair suddenly and unexpectedly lifted from his shoulders, he was on a toot, and who could blame him. How often does a genuine god in a basket come down in your front yard, bearing gifts?

Here was a stand-up guy, old enough and savvy enough to realize that he would be advancing no higher in his church, a fact that he seemed to have accepted with no outward appearance of bitterness or jealousy (who knows what his private thoughts on the matter might have been). He was a hardworking and conscientious parish priest who scrambled to keep his dark and leaky church and his run-down school going, a devout Catholic, but one who saw and did things his own way, thanks very much for all the advice and instruction. Encyclicals, pronouncements, warnings and admonitions from Rome and Boston most urgently and authoritatively communicated cut no ice with him. North Walpole might have been a remote village in Chad for all the attention he paid them; replace me, if you like, and try to find someone better to take my place, if you can. That was where he was coming from. He didn't speak out against his superiors, he quietly ignored them and went his own way.

Most of all, I had come to know him as a man utterly without pretense who did nothing for show, a rare human being without guile or cunning design, with no case to make, no life's argument to pursue, a grown man at peace with himself who knew the difference between right and wrong and was a pleasure to be around. Why can't more of us be like that? It's not that difficult, no matter how driven asshole Daddy was or how neurotic Mommy.

During the few months I had been in town I had come to know this big red-faced, overweight priest pretty well because he hadn't been there that long either and still thought of himself as an outsider. We had that in common. We liked to compare notes on the conduct and habits of the natives over a glass of wine in his rectory kitchen.

Terry Riley was a wonderful, inventive cook, and I dropped by for lunch probably more than I should have because I didn't want to bug Kate, give her the impression I was roaming around the house, spinning my wheels, while she was hard at work in her office.

I poured my friend a neat whiskey, which he accepted and downed, then held out the empty glass for more. "If I pour Father another one, Father won't be able even to crawl home. I'll have to carry Father home over my shoulder," I said.

"Mind your mouth, McFarland, or it's no more free meals you'll be getting from me." He pulled off his sneakers, wet and dirty, and rolled them one by one toward the fireplace. "I'm going to announce the gift Sunday at the nine o'clock, Kate. Maybe you'd like to be there, to see the reaction. They'll all go bananas, believe me. After all, they're your people."

"Yes, and I can hear them now, talking about Mac and me."

"Most of the good ladies of Saint John's think you two slipped off and got secretly married in a civil ceremony somewhere. And when some Nosey Parker asks me about it, I say there is nothing for her to worry about. Which, God knows, is the truth, none of their business."

"But we're not married. That's the fact."

"And do you think I give a damn? That I condemn you?" He was struggling to rise from his seat, and with help from me he made it. "Do you need words from a priest, Kate? Would that help?"

"Steady on," I urged him. I caught him by his right arm and squeezed hard.

He pulled free easily. "You don't know anything about us, Mac. Kate and I are New England Irish Catholic. She needs words said and, by God, I'm going to say them." He spread his arms in invocation. "*In nomine Christi, Amen.*" I glanced at Kate, not at all sure how she was going to take this, but she was sitting with her knees properly together, her hands clasped. Drunk or sober, Terry Riley knew his territory.

The priest fell to his knees. "*Benedicte hunc domum.*" He held his hand out in blessing. "May they live together, Kate and Mac, sharing their love and happiness, forever, as man and woman joined in the eyes of God, with proper religious and civic procedure to follow as soon as possible. *Benedicat vos omnipotens Deus in nomine patris, et filii, et spiritus sancti. Amen.*"

I had to help him to his car and drive him to the rectory. "Mac, I did the best I could," he said on the way before he fell asleep. Kate followed us in her car. "I guess it's better than nothing," she said to me on the way back home.

It didn't satisfy her, of course. Nothing short of marriage ever would. But it was a demonstration, before God, of our intent, and, good old Terry, it bought me a little time.

When Kate got back from the airport I made us a couple of drinks, dark rum and tonic with lots of ice and big wedges of lime. I started a charcoal fire in the grill we kept on the patio, slathered the swordfish steaks with mayonnaise and broiled them. She made a salad and set the table. We sat on the patio, ate and drank a bottle of white wine, and watched the sun go down behind Clam Pond. Then we went to bed.

She was at an age when sexual intercourse has become routine for most women. But I was her first lover, and although she tried to hide it, she was shy and embarrassed by her lack of experience.

There were firm, unstated rules of conduct we followed. We didn't talk about the carnal pleasures awaiting us at the top of the stairs. No hints, no winks, no jokes, no lewd remarks, and no messing around. We were correct and proper, circumspect in every way, as if we were two Victorians at a church picnic.

"I think I'll go up and get a shower," I said after we had cleared the table.

"You go ahead. I'll just start the dishwasher."

I always went upstairs first, undressed, brushed my teeth, showered, and got in bed, with only a small table lamp lighting the room.

Kate followed, walked past me into the bathroom without speaking, blushing and averting her eyes. Her blush never failed to excite me.

A few minutes later she came out wearing a thin white cotton gown, hair shining from the brush, smiling faintly, eyes down, and smelling as sweet as a flower. She crawled in beside me, I turned off the lamp, and she came to me immediately, throwing her arms around my neck and kissing me, as if we had been apart for weeks. Ah, God, sweet love. I wanted to eat her up.

There was no oral sex, no dirty talk, nothing rough or kinky. She liked to hug and kiss silently, with her legs entwined around one of mine. And she liked to decide when I should enter her. She sat up suddenly, pulled off her gown, and fell back on the bed, spreading arms and legs in full welcome, with a big smile on her beautiful face.

It was slow and easy, as always, in the beginning, with light kisses, until, dazed and excited by her growing pleasure, breathing harder and pulling at me, she began to whisper with an open mouth covering my ear, then my mouth, words barely spoken, words I could not compre-

91

hend, exhaling, inhaling sighs and unintelligible sounds of passion and pleasure.

She was all over me, wrapped around me, arms and legs, locked and grunting, until I entered a state of total euphoria and exploded inside her, blown away, out there somewhere. Kate always made it feel like the first time.

When we finished I was covered with sweat and trembling like a leaf while she lay motionless under me, as if she had lapsed into unconsciousness. She liked to lie that way for a few minutes afterwards, until her passion drained away. Sometimes she fell asleep that way, without moving or saying a word to me.

That night I had just about got my breath back when she said, "I assume you and Noah didn't miss the part when Martha was referring to the Bridges subcommittee."

I rolled off her. "Is that what was going through your head? Is that what you were thinking about?"

She slapped me on the stomach. "You know better."

"Noah didn't miss it. He doesn't know what to make of it yet. With everything else happening, I forgot to tell you I'm flying to Phoenix tomorrow with Bridges. A day trip. Maybe he'll say something."

"I did some investigating for you two," she said, a little smugly, I thought. "Martha and I talked on the way to Hyannis, after she'd pulled herself together. She worked at the Capitol herself for a couple of years, before she went into private practice. So she knows her way around the place."

"What did she have to say?"

Kate sat up, found her gown and pulled it over her head. "First of all, it's the Senate Foreign Relations Subcommittee on European Affairs where Susan worked. Its full name. Dolph Bridges was chairman until he left the Senate."

"I could have looked that up in the library."

"I'll pretend I didn't hear that," she said airily. "Susan was part of what they call the support staff, which is a nice way of calling her a clerk."

"There are hundreds of young women like that who work on the Hill." I had never been assigned permanently to Washington, but I had been in and out of the town dozens of times when stories led me there. I knew my way around fairly well.

"As Martha describes it, the entire Foreign Relations Committee staff works in one cluster of offices in the Dirksen office building, thirty people, most of them women and many of them young women. She says all the congressional committee staff offices are meat markets, cattle shows. The Capitol Hill studs are always wandering in, checking out the latest merchandise."

"Did Martha know of any connection between her sister and Bridges or any member of his staff?"

"I didn't ask, to tell you the truth. But Susan must have been in and out of his office suite a lot."

"Did Martha say if Susan ever mentioned Bridges's name, or the name of anybody on his staff?"

"She said once or twice, but nothing personal. Honey,

93

I couldn't pry too much because I didn't know exactly how to handle it, to even mention to Martha the fact that Bridges is up here. She's got a mind like the old steel trap, believe me."

"The only thing we have so far is a connection, that's all. Susan Jacobs worked on Dolph Bridges's Senate subcommittee. The house where he's staying here and the restaurant are separated only by maybe a hundred and fifty yards of water at the Cut. That doesn't add up to much, frankly. It does give Noah reason enough to ask a few questions, that's all."

Kate was sleepy and, I like to think, satisfied and happy. She yawned, laid her head on my shoulder and threw one of her legs over mine. She liked to sleep that way. The late May wind billowed the bedroom curtains softly, the way a light sea breeze billows a mainsail. I could hear the faint movement of animals outside. Rabbits, skunks, foxes, even the small Cape deer foraged the property at night, and I liked the sounds they made.

Sure, there was a connection. I had been on the street too long, covered too many police stories, to think otherwise, even for a moment. Maybe it didn't involve Dolph Bridges or any of the people who worked for him, not directly. But there was a connection, and I would find it. That was what I did best, how I had made a living for twenty-five years. I wondered where it would lead, how it would all end up. I had no idea. Good story, I thought, drifting off to sleep. There's a good story here.

Kate gave me a good-night pat on my chest and I kissed the top of her head. The curtains billowed, the animals outside were on parade, the yard theirs until morning, Kate began to snore softly, and I thought to myself, God, I could live like this forever.

8

I MANAGED TO DRESS AND leave the house early the next morning without waking Kate or the dog Mou-Mou, who somehow always ended up in the bed with her. After a quick stop at Bob's Sandwich Shop for a white-coffee-to-go, I was on the road to Hyannis in my old Ford before first light.

Barnstable County airport was quiet and still when I arrived there, and I found the private jet on the boarding ramp, door open, ready to fly to Phoenix. A young man who looked about the age of an Eagle Scout—okay, a junior assistant scoutmaster, but no older—was walking around the plane with a flashlight, peering at the wings and the fuselage. "Help you?" he asked when I walked out.

I introduced myself and told him I was an added passenger on the flight.

"No problem. Plenty of room. We seat eight. And I'm the driver. Ben Shuler." The air child and I shook hands.

"My crew's gone to an all-night mini-market in town to hustle up some breakfast munchies, including the coffee I can't offer you yet."

"This is a good-looking plane you're flying," I said. The two-engine jet was painted light tan with navy blue trim.

"It's a brand-new Cessna Citation Three," Shuler told me. "It's got AiResearch turbo fan engines. We cruise at four-forty, with coast-to-coast range. And you name the latest, hottest equipment, we got it. It flies itself almost."

"It's a beauty. What does a plane like this go for, anyway?"

"You're looking at six million bucks." When I whistled he held up his hand. "Mr. Munro doesn't own it. You think he's a fool? His company leases it. It's a dry lease, no crew provided. We work for him full time."

"It must cost a fortune to lease a go-go like this."

"Say a hundred and twenty thousand a month."

"I guess you're flying Senator Bridges around about as much as you're flying your boss these days."

"Mr. Munro's usually along."

"You come in this morning from Chicago?"

"Late last night, slept in a motel across the road we use. Mr. Munro stayed with the Senator over in North Walpole. They should be getting here in a few minutes. Get on board if you like. Make yourself at home."

I climbed inside the plane, sat down, checked out the signed picture of the President, and did a little mental

97

arithmetic. Including the crew salary, Charls Munro had to be spending about a million-five for air transportation, and evidently the jet was pretty much at Dolph Bridges's beck and call.

To my knowledge, no other candidate in either party had access to such a splendid, fast-flying machine, and it gave him a big advantage. He could make trips such as this one to Phoenix on only a few hours' notice and at no expense. He could appear at twice as many party functions as his rivals. He could bounce around the country like a Mexican jumping bean.

If and when Bridges got the presidential nomination, the Republican National Committee would take over and he would tour the nation in a big chartered commercial jet, a United M-80 or an American 757, with the reporters who filled the back of the plane, Johnny Apple, Ken Bode, Lou Cannon, the princes of national political news, paying much of the cost, and with a second jet charter of equal size following a few miles behind, the zoo plane, so called because its passengers were the campaign grunts, still photographers, television camera crews, the telephone reps, guys who wore jeans and whose belt buckles were Superman takeoffs that said *Newsman, Truth, Justice and the American Way*. That was the ultimate, the once-in-a-political-lifetime political junket. Meanwhile, the Cessna Citation Three would do just fine. You got to start small and work up.

It was still dark outside, so I found a pillow, let my seat

go back and dozed off. I was dreaming of campaigns past when I was brought out of it with a sharp punch on my shoulder.

"Excuse me, *sir*, but exactly who are *you*?" a young woman asked me. "I don't have a fourth party on my flight manifest."

She was wearing a tan shirtwaist dress and a blue cardigan sweater, the colors of the plane. The name tag on the sweater said *Courtney Morgan*. It was a classy name and too bad God hadn't given her the looks to match. God had given her fat legs, a big ass and a bad complexion.

"Well?" this Courtney Morgan demanded. "I'd like an explanation."

"I guess they forgot to add me to the list."

"What are you, another new staff member? What's your name?"

"I'm not a staff member. I'm a guest of the Senator. Listen, you got any coffee?"

She didn't move. "Unfortunately, there was a recent fatality on the staff, Susan Jacobs, who apparently was found drowned."

I was wide awake now, sure enough. *On the staff?*

"Of course, Susan was a very attractive and very sexy girl, but one with little on-the-job experience or know-how," Courtney said. "She was a clerk-typist, really, and one with very little interest in her work and no career commitment or dedication that I could ever see."

99

"How'd you learn about her death? You're just in from Chicago."

"This morning, at the mini-market, when I went to get stuff for breakfast. I bought a copy of the Cape Cod *Chronicle*, that weekly. I mean, I truly am sorry over Susan's demise and all, but every senior gal on the old Senate staff is going to raise her eyebrows in surprise over that one."

"I guess there must be lots of former Senate staff members who are waiting to join the campaign."

"We're on hold, you might say, until he formally declares and starts working the primary and caucus states. Most of us have found something to tide us over—"

"Is that what this is for you? A temporary job?"

"I don't mind. I flew for a year, Northwest, before I decided to finish college."

"A poly sci major, I bet."

"University of Southern Illinois."

"How long did you work for Dolph in the Senate?"

"Six years. I was listed on the roster as admin, but what I really did was, I liaised with the locals, handled tricky mail. Constituent relations."

"Courtney, I'm writing a profile of him for the *New York Times*. I'd sure like to get together with you and get some human interest stuff, anecdotes, all with his okay, of course."

"I wouldn't mind helping you with that. I know a lot of great anecdotes."

"That's what I was thinking. I'd like to quote you by name, if that's okay."

"Look, I've got hot coffee, real fresh-squeezed orange juice, and there's Danish heating in the oven."

"My friends call me Mac, Courtney."

A live one, I thought as she walked down the aisle to get the food, her big ass bobbing behind her. How precious it is, the very water of life to any news reporter, a news source.

She brought me a tray, then sat across the aisle, crossed her big legs and lit a cigarette. "I don't mind telling you, off the record, Mac, I'm mad enough to spit nails right now."

"You mean the Susan Jacobs thing? Maybe you don't know the real story, being stuck out in Chicago. You being a staff big foot, maybe they have you in mind for bigger things. You'll probably end up as some kind of White House special assistant after the election."

"I intend to be in on this campaign from day one, I guarantee you that."

I knew her type. She was a boiler-room babe, a political groupie. Washington draws into its magnetic field hundreds like her every year. They find politics exciting and challenging, as difficult as that might be for the average, rational person to imagine, and Capitol Hill is their Mecca. To work for a major candidate in a presidential campaign is the ultimate high for them.

Courtney was trying to smoke and bite her nails, what

was left of them, at the same time. "Why Susan Jacobs? Christ, she was off the wall."

"Lights on but nobody home?"

"Not stupid especially. Spacey."

"Sex?"

"I doubt it. Word gets out."

"Maybe she never had a job with Senator Bridges. You don't know for sure, do you?"

Courtney put out her cigarette and found a sliver of nail on her left pinky to rip away. "No, I don't. But then why the hell was she up here?"

It was so early there was no commercial traffic to interrupt our climb; the Citation shot into the sky like a rocket and it was only a few minutes after the takeoff from Hyannis when Ben Shuler, our Romper Room pilot, came on the intercom. "We're leveling off at thirty-five thousand, folks. We've got a six-hour flight ahead of us. That means we should arrive right on time in Phoenix, at ten local time. Enjoy the flight."

Steady as a rock the jet was, and there was a beautiful day dawning behind us as we flew into the last of the night, three men and a woman, all of us still with sleep in our eyes. Dolph, Eliot More and I sat around a table in wide, comfortable leather chairs. Charls Munro sat alone, reading a copy of the *Wall Street Journal*. By unspoken agreement there was no prolonged talk after we all said good morning. Too early for that.

So we sat, drank Courtney's mini-market coffee, which wasn't bad, and read the morning papers. That was fine with me. On a story like that, you usually do better if you don't begin like some hard-nosed panelist on *Meet the Press*.

We made an unlikely quartet. From the looks of us we could have been four strangers in the club car of a train.

I was wearing one of my old off-the-rack Chicago suits that had seen better days and whose best days were not very good, and I wished I had shined my shoes at least because Dolph Bridges was dressed for the national nightly network news in a dark blue suit, white shirt and maroon paisley tie.

Eliot More wore gray linen trousers, a yellow blouse with a Peter Pan collar, and a tan safari jacket. She had a gold charm bracelet on one wrist and a man-sized stainless-steel Rolex on the other. And she had a hard look in her eye for me. Eliot didn't want me on this trip.

Charls Munro was about Dolph's age and everything about him said rich guy, creased designer jeans, persimmon-colored madras shirt, alligator loafers, and a gold watch on one wrist that had a double French-Swiss name I couldn't pronounce and a heavy gold identification bracelet on the other with an engraving on its plate that said *Chas Dos*. Charls Munro II.

I flipped through the morning papers and listened without comment while Dolph and Eliot chatted in political pidgin, commenting on the stories they came across.

Why this candidate was having such a tough time raising money and how that one was having such a hard time trying to run the Senate and run for president at the same time, how this one was too short and that one was too boring and still another one was too intelligent for his own good.

"Like Stevenson," Eliot More said. "Can you imagine him trying to run for president today?"

"I see God's been talking to the Ayatollah again," Dolph said, referring to a religious fundamentalist who had announced he was thinking about running for the Republican nomination. "I wish He'd give me a buzz sometime."

"Do you think he's going to run?" I asked.

"Does Annie love Sandy?" Eliot asked. "He's got a staff of thirty-five people working full time on it."

Dolph folded his newspaper and slapped it on the table. "It must sound to Mac here like we're handicapping a horse race."

"That's really what it comes down to, isn't it?"

"In a way." Dolph lifted his empty cup and Courtney was at his side in a flash to refill it. "Most people don't understand the process or give a damn," he said. "Every four years there's a Republican and a Democrat running for president, and the voter picks one of them. People vote on hunch and gut instinct, in my opinion."

"The hard part is getting it boiled down to a choice between two people," Eliot said. "The general election is a dash. The nominating process is a race through an obstacle course."

All I knew about Eliot More was what I had read in the library. She was a Courtney Morgan who had made it. She had spent a couple of years at the Republican National Committee trying to convince college kids that Gerald Ford was a hell of a guy. Then she set up her own consulting firm. Yo, my man, how to round up those kids, the baby boomers, the yuppies, the young new collars, that was her specialty, and she proved good at it. She had not yet managed a losing campaign.

There is no way to measure the true worth of a consultant such as she in most elections. If a candidate is good enough he doesn't need help, and if he's that bad no fast gun can save him. But these people have become political vanity items as well as signs of serious intent. When a candidate brought someone of Eliot More's standing on board it meant he was not fooling around.

She ran Dolph's political action committee, Proud America, which, through political metamorphosis, would become his campaign staff. She had all the names and the figures, she hired and fired, said yes and no, subject only to Dolph's veto. And like most of her kind, she was sure she alone knew the secret path that led to the White House.

"People who vote in Republican primaries are more conservative than average Republicans. That's the problem," she said to me.

"Which means Dolph's got to keep his opponents from pushing him to the left."

"Look at Jerry Ford. He was president and he almost lost the nomination to Reagan in 1976 because Reagan occupied the right."

"So I've got to win the nomination and then turn around in the general election and convince mainstream voters I'm not a right-wing nut," Dolph said.

"Governor Gould's decision won't hurt you," I said.

"Mac, I've got to win the Iowa caucus *and* the New Hampshire primary. Prove I'm a vote getter in the North and then head South."

"He'll go to every Southern state, spend to the limit, and hope to come in a strong second. Then the Midwest is next and Dolph's their kind of Republican. That's where he'll win the nomination," Eliot said.

"My problem is in the South," Dolph said. "Television's the only way and that's going to cost big money. How much, Charlie?"

"Five million minimum," Charls Munro said, not looking up from his newspaper. "Don't worry. We'll find the money."

"We need it pretty soon. We've got to hire a good agency and start preparing the television ads," Eliot said. "They don't take credit cards, not after the way they got burned in '84."

"That's my job."

"You sound pretty sure of yourself, Mr. Munro," I

said. "With so many candidates, there's not that much money to go around."

Munro folded his newspaper. "I'm backing a winner and in politics a winner attracts money."

"Charlie and I were college classmates," Dolph told me.

Munro pointed his finger at Dolph. "You're looking at Mr. University of Illinois."

"Listen to him," Dolph said. "He really ran things."

"The world is filled with insiders," Munro said to me. "We're guards and tackles who clear the way, that's all. Dolph is an All-American running back."

Dolph groaned. "Charlie."

"I mean it. You'll have what you need. I'll see to that."

"There is such a thing as the Federal Election Commission," I said.

"To hell with them. To hell with all these reforms. They've screwed up the way we elect presidents in this country if you ask me." He reached across the aisle and gave Dolph a pat on the knee. "Don't worry, I'm not going to break any laws."

Dolph gave me a long and serious look that said *I need him*. He's an old, loyal friend. He's not going to be my secretary of the treasury. I'll ship him off to be ambassador to Ireland or somewhere. But right now I need him, need this jet, his contacts, and all the rest. So get off my back. All this Dolph's look told me.

I decided to play along and not make waves. "I've read

a lot about you," I told Munro. "I used to work in Chicago. You're a great community servant there."

"I guess I've become that. My wife's the joiner. I just pay the bills, the symphony, the art museum."

"And now Senator Bridges. And all you'll get out of it is the satisfaction of seeing him in the White House. Maybe an invitation to a state dinner now and then."

"You may be sure I would call on Charlie for advice and counsel when things got hot," Dolph said.

Eliot More looked as if she wanted to throw me out of the plane without a chute. "In this presidential rat race, every candidate needs a friend," she said.

"Boy, isn't that the truth," I said.

"Fasten your seat belts, folks," the boy pilot said on the intercom. "We're running into a little unexpected clear-air turbulence here."

9

I T DIDN'T TAKE LONG. We knew something had gone wrong the moment Dolph got back to the airport after his meeting with Governor Ray Gould.

We had landed at Sky Harbor International right on time, and we found Fred Dingell, the young state senator who served as Dolph's county chairman, waiting for us at the charter terminal. No reporters, no rented limos, no hoopla of any kind. Dingell, who looked like the Marlboro cowboy's kid brother, was alone, driving his own car, following to the letter the instructions Thomas Duncan had given him.

Dingell told us that Governor Gould had agreed to a short private meeting, fifteen or twenty minutes, with Dolph in his office. He also said the governor's decision to pull out of the race was the talk of the town and of the entire state, for that matter. Gould, after all, was their boy, and the people of Arizona had wanted him to run for president to show the rest of the nation the sort of young leader the state was producing.

His surprise withdrawal was still big national news. Dingell told us there were three or four television tape camera crews in town, rushed in from Los Angeles the minute the announcement was made. They were all staked out in the hallway of the state capitol, outside the governor's office suite, smoking and putting the butts out on the marble floor, drinking Cokes and leaving the empty cans on the walnut tables, reading and discarding newspapers, and generally making a mess for the janitors to clean up and complain about.

Every political columnist and editorial writer had commented about the withdrawal. Gould didn't have the taste for it, they wrote. He had to take care of his children. He had trouble raising money. The big boys in the party had said *Wait until next time.* Not a word, not an intimation about AIDS. Either nobody had figured it out or nobody wanted to write about it.

Dingell, who obviously mistook me for another staff member, said he had quietly put out the word to the camera crews about Dolph's visit. "On my own, of course. I told them, Dolph Bridges wants this to be a strictly private visit and he would skin me alive if he learned I let you boys in on it. But what the hell, I said, I figure it's legitimate news."

A good man, young Dingell, who knew how to think on his feet. Eliot More nodded her head in approval and Dolph gave him a pat on his back. Did we have here a potential Arizona state chairman, perhaps even a Southwestern area campaign coordinator?

They left, just the two of them, in Dingell's Plymouth, for the state capitol. A white Cadillac with shaded windows, a uniformed chauffeur and a young man with a briefcase picked up Charls Munro to take him to Scottsdale for a look-see at a shopping center that was in trouble and for sale. Eliot, the crew members and I waited in the departure lounge. The crew sat around a table in the small restaurant, drinking iced tea; I spent the time writing in my small notebook some of the things that had been said on the plane, and Eliot worked the pay phone.

Every good national political organizer I have known can set up shop simply by finding a phone and opening a briefcase, and Eliot was a good one. She was never off the phone from the moment Dolph left the airport until he came stalking into the charter lounge alone less than an hour later.

"Let's get the hell out of here. *Now*," he snapped.

"Munro's not back yet," Eliot told him.

"Then he can damn well take a commercial jet. I said now."

As if on cue, Charls Munro pulled up in his Cadillac, shook hands with the young man who carried the briefcase, and entered the terminal. Eliot rounded up the crew and we boarded the beautiful Citation. Dolph took his seat, buckled up and stared out his window, not saying another word.

"Okay, let's go. Back to Hyannis. Move it," Eliot shouted through the open cockpit door. Something had gone terribly wrong but she wasn't about to ask what it was. I've seldom seen an angrier man than Dolph was at that moment.

Courtney Morgan, who hadn't caught on, came forward, glass in hand. "My, you look like you could use some iced tea, Senator. And I've got some delicious crabmeat salad for lunch when you want it."

Dolph didn't look at her, made no reply, so she placed the glass carefully on the table before him. "Also some of that cherry yogurt you like."

The engines were started, we taxied out to the flight line, and after a short wait that seemed like an eternity, we were given clearance and roared down the runway.

"Courtney, you can bring me a gin and tonic," Charls Munro said. He stretched out, placing his feet on an empty chair. "While you people were playing at politics, I stoled me a little holding company today, a shopping center, and three, count them, three office buildings, plus an old orange grove on Indian School Road I'm going to have myself some fun with. Not a bad hour's work for yours truly."

"That's really nice, Mr. Munro," Courtney said, serving him his drink.

Eliot More waited until we leveled off at flight altitude. "Obviously it didn't go well, Dolph. May I ask what happened?"

"I saw him, alone, just the two of us. I told him I happened to be out West on other business and this was a personal drop-in visit. The reporters and the camera crews were waiting for me at the car when I left. I told them the same thing and I'm pretty sure the dumb bastards bought it."

"So what exactly is the problem?" Eliot asked.

"No problem. If you don't count the fact that the son of a bitch spat in my face."

"Jesus! Dolph!"

"What's this all about?" Munro asked.

Crazy Courtney ventured forward. "A long drink of that iced tea will do wonders for you, Senator. I made it myself in the sun, on the wing of the plane."

"Gould knew you knew," Eliot said. "He found out somehow."

"He knew it or guessed it," Dolph said. "I never got the chance to tell him how truly sorry I am for his misfortune. He told me he knew why I was there. He called me a filthy bloodsucker. Then he spat in my face and told me to get out of his office."

"I know people in Arizona. I'll have his ass for breakfast," Munro shouted.

"He's got AIDS, Charlie," Dolph told him.

"I don't give a shit if he's got leprosy."

"Is there any chance he'll leak the fact that he spat on you?" Eliot asked.

"I don't think so. After he did it, he sat down at his desk, put his face in his hands and started crying."

"I'm sorry, Dolph." Eliot reached over and placed her hand on his knee. "It was my call and I'm sorry."

"I'm never going to put myself in a situation like that again."

That was when Courtney got into it. If she had had the brains of a monkey, she would have opened the plane door and climbed out on one of the wings to keep out of it, but Courtney did not possess such smarts. "This is exactly why you need me on the staff, Senator," she said. "You need my expertise to liaise with people like that and it never would have happened." She had tears in her eyes, her bottom lip was quivering and she was swaying back and forth slightly, but her fists were clenched. "Please? Before something like this happens again?"

"What? What is it?" I think he believed she was offering him a drink or something.

"I can liaise, Senator. I can coordinate, put things like this together. No problems, no misunderstandings."

"The Senator does know that, Courtney," Eliot said quietly.

"There's too much at stake here. For you and those of us who believe in your cause," Courtney said. She was struggling to retain some control over her emotions, but it seemed to me she had less than a fifty-fifty chance of making it. I felt sorry for her because all she really wanted to be was a good Indian warrior, not a chief, and she was destroying whatever chance she had of being that.

"The Senator appreciates your loyalty, Courtney. We all do," Eliot said.

"He needs a scheduler," Courtney told her. "It's come down to that and today proves it. That's one of the things I happen to be very good at."

"We're aware of that. We do have plans for you along that line later in the campaign," Eliot said.

"I think you ought to bring me on board now. If I'd been in place, this never would have happened. Whatever it was."

"We'll get together in the next few days and talk about it," Eliot said with a slight smile and I wondered where Courtney was going to find work.

Courtney smiled through her tears. "You won't regret it, Eliot. I'm that extra pair of hands you need and don't even know it. Once I'm aboard, you'll wonder how you ever did without me."

"I'm sure you're right," Eliot said. "Now, why don't you make us a fresh pot of coffee?"

"You name it, you got it. Everything from fresh coffee to a status report on Alaska. I mean, I certainly can understand how you would need somebody like Susan Jacobs to help out with filing and typing and such in the early stages. An extra pair of hands. But you talk Courtney Morgan, you're talking about a *big* pair of extra hands, my friend." Big mouth, too.

Eliot smiled and it nearly caused me to shiver. "What about Susan Jacobs? I don't understand you, Courtney."

Dolph was listening now. "I don't either," he said.

He and Eliot exchanged the briefest of glances. *Something,* I thought. *Something between them.*

Charls Munro also had been listening. "Maybe the job Courtney ought to have is travel coordinator. That way, I could pick up her salary," he said. "If you're worrying about budget."

"What about Susan Jacobs?" Dolph asked Courtney, ignoring Munro.

"It's only that I am personally very, very saddened over Susan's passing on so suddenly and unexpectedly. But you have to admit yourself that she was strictly a gofer, period."

"Are you under the impression she was on the campaign staff, working in North Walpole?" Eliot asked. That smile again.

"Why else would she have been in town?"

"Courtney, we don't know. None of us," Eliot said. "The first time any of us knew she was in North Walpole was when we read about her death."

"Dolph, what I didn't know was that Susan Jacobs used to work for you," I said. Let him figure out how I had learned that.

"Courtney, I think I'm ready for that crabmeat salad now," Dolph said. After she rushed to comply, he turned to me. "You got it wrong. She didn't work for me."

"She worked for one of Dolph's subcommittees when he was in the Senate," Eliot said to me. "Dolph didn't hire her. Dolph didn't supervise her work. Dolph didn't know her, except maybe as a face in the crowd."

Dolph Bridges smiled. Hand in the cookie jar. "Mac, what we have here is a little cover-up."

"Really? Gee, that's interesting. Tell me about it."

Charls Munro stood up, stretched and walked forward. "Whistle when the crabmeat salad's served. I'm going to watch them fly my plane for a while. I'm trying to figure out why I pay them so much money."

"Eliot, you go back to the galley and keep that maniac woman occupied while Mac and I talk," Dolph said.

"She'll want on the payroll," Eliot said.

"Then put her on. Send her out to organize Idaho or something."

"I'll have to give her a title. And a good salary."

"If you have to, do it." He turned to me. "Mac, you can see where I have a problem with this young woman's death."

"I can see where you have a very big problem."

"I don't know why she was in North Walpole. I didn't even know she *was* there."

"And there she was, living in a restaurant dormitory a hundred and fifty yards away from the house where you're staying, right across the Cut. Another Chappaquiddick. That's what you're worried about, isn't it?"

"You're damn right I am. So is Eliot. Mac, it's guilt by association. Susan Jacobs worked on my old subcommittee. I'm told she was young and good-looking. Therefore, I was involved with her. Or, at least, every damn paper in the country will put a reporter on the story full time and try to prove I was."

"And you've decided to try and stonewall it."

"We're doing our damnedest to put distance between us. We're not volunteering any information. All we're doing is telling the simple truth, when we're asked questions."

"And you want me to keep my mouth shut?"

"Unless you want to see me go down for something I had nothing to do with. All it would take is a spark to set off a forest fire."

"I'm not on any mission, if that's what you're getting at."

"I can't afford any speculation, no gossip, no rumor. Look what it did to Kennedy."

"You're placing me in a hell of a situation here, Dolph."

"I'm not claiming I'd be a great president. But name me a guy who'd make a better one. At least I deserve the chance for a clean shot at it."

Courtney came to set the table. "Oh, Senator, you won't regret this, I promise you," she said, sniffing and wiping away a last remaining tear. "Eliot says you want me to start Monday on the overseas delegates. And, boy, sir, am I going to work my buns off for you."

"Good. That's just fine. Those overseas delegates are so often overlooked. But in a tight race like this one, they can be the difference between winning and losing."

We were flying high above the weather in the Citation

and the flat brown and green of the Southwest was moving below us.

"You may have a bigger problem than you realize," I said. "If it came down to it, can you prove where you were on Tuesday night, the night Susan Jacobs was murdered?"

He stared at me. "Who says she was murdered?"

"The North Walpole police chief suspects she was."

"Jesus, that's all I need, for him to start making waves."

"I don't think he has, not yet."

"What's he come up with?"

"Susan Jacobs's body was found in the front passenger's seat, Dolph. Everything points to a second person being involved. And the chief knows she worked on the staff of your old Senate subcommittee."

"You haven't printed any of this?"

"Not yet."

"Hold off. That's what I'm asking."

A smiling Courtney, now fully recovered, served us the crab salad and poured white wine. "Eliot and I are munching together, making campaign plans," she said happily.

The crab salad was quite good. I knew Dolph Bridges was waiting for me to speak.

I hate it when reporters try to play God. Usually it causes trouble in the end. But I wasn't employed full time by a newspaper anymore. I was a free-lancer, a lowly stringer, and, thus, a news blockade runner, somewhat free to cross borders.

Noah Simmons had asked me to hold off and not screw up his investigation. Dolph Bridges was asking me to hold off and give him the benefit of the doubt.

"I'll hold off as long as I can," I said.

10

"I ALWAYS GET LOST ON the Cape," Helen Bridges said to me. "All these little roads running in all directions to all these little towns."

"And to add to the confusion, there's the North, South, East, West problem," I said. "Yarmouth, South Yarmouth, West Yarmouth. I can't keep them straight, either."

"Before I leave the house I sit down with a map and plot myself a route."

She seemed pleasant enough. We were heading west, the two of us, with her at the wheel, on Route 6, the mid-Cape expressway, on our way to Osterville. She was driving a red Jeep Wagoneer, which came with the house.

Helen Bridges would have turned the head of any man half her age who saw her whizzing by in that Wagoneer. Her face had not a wrinkle or a sag, not a hint of a crow's-foot around her eyes, and as we rode down the highway, between the small dying brown pines, I searched for the telltale sign of a face-lift, that slightly Oriental look not uncommon for a woman her age, but it wasn't there.

She wore a tan-colored Hermès scarf tied over her head, a white cotton sweater with the sleeves pushed up over her elbows, tailored jeans and tan loafers, no jewelry except a gold wedding ring and a Cartier tank watch. Helen Bridges was a classy-looking woman who took very good care of herself.

She took a quick glance at the instructions she had written on a three-by-five card, turned off Route 6 and headed south on 149 toward Marston Mills.

"Thanks for letting me tag along," I said.

"I don't know what you expect to get out of it."

"I don't know you. I'm trying to get a fix on you. That's all. The *Times* profile I'm doing, well, it's important to Dolph."

"So he's told me. Not to mention Billy Nolan."

"It's a salute of respect by the paper, their way of saying he's a serious candidate, in their opinion."

I had told Billy I needed a one-on-one interview with her for the article, and he had called me at eight o'clock that morning to say Helen was going on a shopping trip at ten and I could go along if I liked.

Nothing more had occurred on the return trip from Phoenix the evening before. There was no more talk about the death of Susan Jacobs.

When Billy called, Kate and I were eating breakfast, if that's the word for it, half a grapefruit, one piece of dry toast, black coffee. We were trying, off and on, to diet, and that morning Kate announced we were on again.

She didn't need to lose weight, but she was the kind of woman who moaned about how fat she was getting if the bathroom scales showed the gain of a single pound. I'll admit it's a different story with yours truly.

"Maybe we can find a cup of coffee in Osterville," I said to Helen Bridges after we had gone through Marston Mills, which didn't take long. "Couple of doughnuts or something."

She said nothing but glanced at my stomach, which managed to get her message across.

"Okay, I need to lose about fifteen pounds. I always need to lose about fifteen pounds. God made me fifteen pounds overweight," I said.

"I'm not a diet nut. But I feel better if I let my body dictate its needs, not my taste buds, Mr. McFarland."

I didn't especially appreciate the constant use of *mister*. Tony women use the title to address men of minor station.

"You're going to be another Jackie Kennedy," I said. "My."

"Dolph becomes president, you'll be queen of America." Oh, I was spooning it on, rich and thick, because I knew everybody likes to hear that kind of talk, but I also meant what I said. "Have you thought about it at all? What kind of First Lady would you be?"

We were just outside Osterville. She turned the Jeep off the road, into the lot of a specialty shop, braked to a stop and turned off the engine.

"Is this the place?" I asked.

"No. I want to talk. Frankly, you frighten me, Mr. McFarland."

"I don't mean to, Mrs. Bridges."

"I've had very little experience dealing with people like you."

"You better get used to it. When this campaign really starts, you're going to be under siege. I'm a piece of cake. Wait until the Sally Quinns of this world come calling."

"I won't answer. Since he and I have been married I've managed to avoid that."

"Unless you want to hurt your husband you're going to have to play the game. There is no escape. A lot has been written about you already."

"I know that. But with as little cooperation from me as possible. I hate it, all of it."

"Has anything been written that's grossly inaccurate? Anything you want to set me straight on?"

She thought about it. "No, not that's inaccurate. Oh, a few little things. It's just silly."

"If Dolph is nominated, every detail of your life is going to come out. Like, where'd you go to college? What was your first husband like? How did you and

Dolph meet? Were there any serious men in between? And on and on."

"I see your point. Others have warned me."

"And it scares you."

"It scares the hell out of me. I'm not a political person, you see."

"What are you, then? You're married to a politician, after all."

"I see my first and greatest responsibility as being a good wife to my husband. I love him. If he's elected president, so be it. If not, I'll go right on."

"There's a little more to it than that. From what I've read, you're society Washington, the daughter of an old Washington family. You and Dolph live out in the Virginia hunt country. Your first husband was really rich. Reporters are going to be crawling all over you."

"That's really none of your concern, is it?"

Okay. I let fly with my curveball. "Mrs. Bridges, did you know Susan Jacobs?"

Her face told me nothing. "The young woman who was drowned? No, I never met her, although I understand she was a clerk on one of Dolph's old subcommittees. She'd been drinking heavily and taking some kind of dope, hadn't she?"

Yes, she had. But to my knowledge, nobody had said anything about that yet, not publicly.

"Why do you ask?" A casual question. Either she knew nothing or she was a member of the team whose game plan was to keep a tight lid on this thing. I didn't know which.

"I'm also a stringer for the Boston *Globe*. I'm doing the story and I need all the details I can get. I thought your paths might have crossed."

"I'm sorry, no. I didn't know the young woman. There are lots like her in Washington, of course."

In Osterville we found a parking spot on Main Street and went into Eldred Wheeler's, a very good antiques shop. They had a flat-top highboy, c. 1750–1780, ten thousand dollars. She told me she had seen a picture of it in *Cape Cod Life* and wanted to take a look at it for herself. She did, examined it with the eye of an expert, and pronounced it worth the price. "It'd bring twice that in Washington," she told me. Next we went into Churchill's, where she spotted a model sailing ship in a fat gray bottle. Seven hundred bucks. "Too much for me," she said.

From Osterville we drove back to North Walpole. "I'm in the market for a house gift for the Munros," she told me on the way. "The ship in the bottle was simply too expensive. Now I'm thinking about a quarter board for the pool house, and I think I may have found one."

Quarter boards are hand-carved wooden identification plaques taken from wrecked and sunken ships and they are greatly prized on the Cape. *Aransas*. *Martha A. Berry*. *Corncrib*. *Praise Ye The Lord*. *Cora E. Cressy*. People liked to mount them over fireplaces in dens and over barn and garage doors. There are wood-carving shops that make reproductions, but authentic quarter boards are hard to come by. Cost you a pretty penny, too.

"How'd you find somebody with a real quarter board he's willing to part with?" I asked.

"Thomas Duncan found him, some Cape Cod chap who's Dolph's Barnstable County campaign chairman. A local lawyer named Bascombe Midgeley. Thomas describes him as a country squire type."

Indeed. The country squire was waiting when we arrived at his home. The quarter board over his garage door said *Mildred A. Simpson*, faint gold lettering on a long piece of faded black wood. The country squire saluted us in greeting.

Some woman was there also, standing in the driveway with a cameraman and a sound engineer. "You hoo, babe," she called out.

"Oh, Christ, Christ, *Christ*," the possible future First Lady exclaimed. "How did she get up here? What am I ever going to do?" The woman ran up to the Jeep and the two of them embraced warmly, as if they were reunited sisters.

"Helen! How *are* you?"

"Lala! It's been *ages*."

"You look terrific!"

"You don't look a day older. I see you all the time on television."

"*Beautiful People*. I'm here in North Walpole to make

you famous. Billy arranged it, and, I'm sure, didn't tell you about it. Who's this hunk?"

Helen introduced us and Lala Powers looked me over from head to toe, taking her time about it, as if I were up for sale and she was deciding whether to buy, a hard choice.

Not that it mattered. I would have turned and run. There did not seem to be much of the original Lala Powers left. You had your bleached hair, your obvious face-lift and, I thought, maybe a nose chop as well because it was a little too pert. You had your layered makeup, your false eyelashes, and I would have bet your silicone breasts as well because when she walked there was no jiggle.

Add to all the above white skintight jeans, spike heels, gray aviator shades, bright ceramic earrings, a canary-yellow sweater, and what you got was Lala. Everything about her said New York City, that one-thing-too-much look. Pull off and scrape away all the layers, and I would guess she was about Helen's age, in her early forties, but my impression was that Lala Powers was caught in a time warp, a woman who considered herself to be perpetually thirty-three.

"Whoever you are, haul your ass out of the car, big boy," she said to me. "I'll deal with you later."

I would have liked to say something smart and sharp, but I didn't try. I simply looked at her.

"Come on, move it, asshole," she said. "We have to

take some pictures. It's snapshot time. Helen, we're doing a full profile piece on you for *Beautiful People*, five, six minutes." She turned and waved her cameraman over. "This is Juno."

All white he was, skin as white as ivory, white sneakers and socks, white duck trousers, a white polo shirt, a white goatee, and two tufts of white hair separated by a bald, sun-reddened scalp, the only color to him.

"He's Hungarian, or something," Lala said. "I think he sucks blood. If you got a cross on you, get it out."

The all-white cameraman took Helen's hand in his, bowed and kissed it. "Juno Vlados, modom. Is great pleasure."

"For a second there I thought he was going to sink his fangs in and take a blood break," Lala said.

Juno laughed. His teeth were white, too. "Only vhen moon is full. Lala makes joke, joke, joke all the time. Modom Bridges, you are beautiful voman and ve vant make you look extra good. So ve ask, please, reshoot you drive in here."

"He sounds like Jack Benny playing Karl Marx and he looks like a hungry vampire, but he knows what he's doing," Lala said.

"Exactly what is it you want me to do?" Helen asked.

"No staging!" Vlados cried, raising a clenched fist. "Juno Vlados never stage. You, man, get out. Ve don't know who you are and Lala here has no time explain you. You, modom, go out, drive in again, my signal. Ve do couple takes, maybe. Make editor happy. I myself do not get fired."

I got out of the Jeep, left them to their business, walked over and joined Bascombe.

Bascombe wore costumes, not clothes, costumes according to his whim. One day he would be costumed as the Harvard-educated New England lawyer in a conservative blue suit and black cap-toed Church's shoes, the next as an Irish country squire in baggy tweeds. Today he was Paddington Bear in the country, wearing stout walking shoes from L. L. Bean, fawn-colored plus fours, gray knee-length stockings, and a sweater and cap. All that was lacking was a tag around his wrist that said *Please Take Good Care of This Bear*.

"I had no idea you were so actively involved in politics," I said.

"Old cock." We shook hands. I liked Bascombe Midgeley, loved him, in fact. My darts partner appeared at times—okay, most times—to be a pompous Anglophile, vain and stuffy, but he really had a dry wit, a good brain, a keen eye and a generous heart. He was the son of a local clergyman so poor he had to clerk part time at the hardware store to make ends meet.

"I didn't know you had decided to cast your lot with Dolph Bridges," I said.

"A good man. He's a moderately conservative Republican, as I am. And he has a chance of winning. Barnstable County is Republican territory, you know, Mac."

"Do I sense a little political ambition here, Bascombe?"

"Maybe two or three terms as the Cape's congressman. I admit the thought has crossed my mind. I'd make a damn good congressman for this district."

"I never said you wouldn't. I'd vote for you."

"If you were registered here."

"And you'd give away your quarter board to further your political career?"

He glanced up at *Mildred A. Simpson*, which usually occupied a place of honor over the fireplace in his den. Now he had it nailed above the garage door. "I found it on the beach when I was a kid, thirteen."

"As I understand it, Helen Bridges is going to give it to Charls Munro's wife as a house gift, for her to nail on the side of a poolside cabana. Can you live with that?"

"If the price is right, old cock, she can screw it on the front bumper of that Jeep. It's one of the ways we make ends meet on the Cape, remember. Off summer people."

Helen Bridges had driven the car into Bascombe's driveway a second time as Juno Vlados had requested, and now he wanted her to do it yet again. "This time Juno on ground vit camera. You pull up, stop, beautiful lady, pebbles fly, very dramatic picture vhich make editor very happy. But careful you not crush poor Juno."

Helen sighed but did it again, stopping the car about six inches short of the camera lens. The albino Hungarian jumped to his feet. "Stop! Don't open door until

Juno say." He stepped back and to one side, his camera on his shoulder, his sound engineer beside him. An electrical cord connected the camera to the cassette color tape recorder the engineer carried. "Okay, open door, get out, valk over, shake gentleman's hand. And please, both of you, do not look camera, smile, say you on candid camera."

The shot was made. "Stop!" Vlados shouted. "Don't none of you say verd until I get position." He got behind Bascombe so he could shoot over Bascombe's shoulder. "Now, Juno say go, beautiful lady, you walk up, shake hands, maybe you say good morning, gentleman, how much money you vant this sign."

With the tape camera rolling, Helen walked up to Bascombe. "Good day," she said. "I'm interested in your quarter board."

"Sorry, it's not for sale."

"What the fuck is this?" Lala Powers shouted.

"Bascombe Midgeley here, Mrs. Bridges," Bascombe said with a quick bow of his head. "It occurs to me you might be making a mistake here. This is an authentic quarter board off an old coal ship. There aren't many of them around. Most are in Cape Cod museums. This one is worth, I would say, about four thousand dollars."

"Oh, dear," Helen said. "I had no idea."

"No, no," Vlados cried. "On camera. We must think of camera."

"Doesn't that make for an image problem?" Bascombe

said. "People all over the country will be seeing you talking about paying four thousand dollars for what looks like an old piece of wood with a woman's name carved on it. I think it would appear a bit ostentatious."

"The man has a point," I said.

"We need a picture," Lala Powers said. "So you two talk about the damn thing, about how old and rare it is, something."

"Better still, Mr. Bascombe here—"

"Midgeley. Bascombe Midgeley."

"He could tell me how much it's worth and I could throw up my hands and say forget it," Helen said.

"And I could advise you to look around for an old reproduction," Bascombe said. "They're much less expensive."

"Cute. That'll work," Lala said. "It'll show people how careful you are with money, Helen."

"Isn't that called staging?" I asked, regretting it as soon as I said it.

"Teeny bit," Juno said. "Teeny weeny bit staging. But innocent, no deception, not changing essential facts."

"And while we're at it, why don't you get lost," Lala added.

"Come on, Mac. Damn it," Bascombe said. He wanted to be on the telly with Helen Bridges.

Juno shot the scene every which way, again and again, hands, close-ups of faces, wide shots. Bascombe proved to be an excellent actor, a quick study, stronger in his role and more natural and convincing with each retake. And Helen was equally good, patient and accommodating, even when the all-white Hungarian, dusty and dirty now from all the crawling around, asked for a fourth and final retake.

Helen didn't strike me as someone shy and anxious to avoid publicity. She looked like the good political wife who was playing the game. After all, Dolph was not exactly running for county dogcatcher.

After they completed the sequence, the two women plotted the rest of the day's shoot. I was sort of left by the wayside, free to tag along if I liked. Television.

Lala wanted pictures of her playing tennis, and Helen said fine, she would ask Thomas Duncan to rally with her. Lala clapped her hands in delight and said Thomas's fab bod would excite her female viewers and the color of his skin wouldn't exactly hurt Dolph's chances with the boogie vote.

Lala wanted pictures of Helen swimming in the pool, or, even better, walking down and diving off the dock into the Cut. Juno wanted to shoot it from a boat, out in the water. "A little bit tasty cheese cake never hurt," a beaming Juno said.

Lala finally said she wanted pictures of Helen working in the library at a desk, proper and all dressed up, serious, reading something, the goddamn phone book for all she cared, and Helen said okay but she wanted a hairdresser to come over from Hyannis.

Then, Lala said, they could do the interview, and Helen said sure, but would it be okay if Lala went over the questions with her in advance? "No problem, babe," Lala said.

Helen didn't appear to be upset by this mini–media blitz. I had warned her that reporters were going to be crawling all over her, which Lala was now doing, but Helen didn't seem to mind, even though she had muttered "Christ, Christ, Christ" when she first spotted Lala.

A smart woman with a mind like a computer, I decided. When you thought you had her number, the number changed. And how did she know Susan Jacobs had been drinking and using?

11

"THE HELL YOU MEAN you got no table for us!" Billy Nolan was shouting. "What do I see, I look about? See all around there? I am looking at one dozen or more empty tables is what I am looking at, and one of them is ours."

Billy's wrath was directed at the young maître d', who was stationed at the entrance of the Cranberry House restaurant, a slender young man, maybe twenty, black trousers, white shirt, black bow tie, a head of bleached blond hair and a face that told you this was opening night and he was new on the job. "Sir, they're all reserved. I swear it," he said.

"All reserved, my ass. Any restaurant charges the prices this one does always holds back a few tables in case some big shot shows up. You think I don't know that?"

"Good evening, Herbie," Kate said to the young man, who looked as if he wanted to fall on his knees and hug her when she and I walked in.

Kate and I had decided, this being opening night, to go out for dinner, her treat. It's only money, hers. She had insisted she could put it on her expense account. I knew she wouldn't but I didn't argue. When we walked inside, we found Billy standing at the entrance with Lala Powers and Thomas Duncan. I performed the introductions.

"You got any pull in this joint? We need a table," Billy said to me.

"It's my first time here, also. Sorry."

"Cranberry House is one of the most popular restaurants on the Cape and it's tough when you don't reserve," Kate said. "And on top of everything else, this is opening night."

"It's a madhouse, Mrs. Bingham," the young maître d' said. "Four waiters and one of the cooks didn't show up for work. Mr. Loory is out in the kitchen, cooking himself. He said to tell you the junkie you sent him is at work."

"Good. The kid needs a break. He's trying to quit using."

"You got one of the best tables in the house. Mr. Loory said. Over by the window."

"I'm impressed," I told Kate.

Kate glanced at the table, then at me, and I gave her a *Why not* with my eyes. "It's a table for four, Mac," she said. "I'm sure they could squeeze in a fifth setting, if your friends would like to join us."

They quickly agreed. "Anything to shut Billy up. He was about to punch the poor kid out," Lala said.

Lala was dressed as a Victorian teenage schoolgirl, in white starched linen with bow, bleached hair tied back in a ponytail with a baby blue silk ribbon. It took a lot of raw courage on her part even to try it.

The table was more than large enough for the five of us and the view was perfect. There was a clear sky, a half-moon, and across the way we could see the Munro House, its lawns and gardens, the dock and the pool all softly lit up. The patio off the sun porch was illuminated by torches fueled by kerosene, and we could, at that distance, clearly see the Bridges and the Munros dining together at a table there.

I winked at Kate and gave her a quick hug of thanks, which brought a smile. She knew who these people were because I tended to tell her almost everything. I could also tell she was pleased to have received such immediate, favored service from Herbie, to have solved so quickly, with only a few words and a dazzling smile, the dining problem of these friends of mine, these *tourists*. After all, this was her turf.

Cranberry House had pickled-pine walls, gray carpeting, recessed ceiling lighting, cane-back chairs and white tablecloths. In a far corner, a pianist in black tie was playing, what else, Porter and Gershwin. Our waitress approached our table, a young college girl, red face, red arms and legs, who had spent too much time in the sun that day and, no doubt, was living upstairs in the waitress dorm where Susan Jacobs had slept. "Good evening. My name is Jennifer—"

"Double Irish neat here," Billy snapped at her. "You know what that means? No ice. Draft beer chaser on the side. Her, vodka tonic." That was Lala. "Them, anything they want, my tab." That was Kate and I. "And him, separate check. Because I ain't buying so much as a glass of water for this chocolate-covered asshole." That was Thomas.

Had our Billy boy been drinking, drinking a lot? Does Howdy Doody have wooden balls? With Thomas's nod of approval, I ordered a bottle of white wine for the three of us, a house specialty Kate knew about and recommended. It was bottled in California by a friend of the owner. Jennifer got out of there. Billy burped, loudly and without apology.

"Do me a big favor," Lala said to him sweetly. "Please try to act a teeny bit more civilized and a little less vulgar now that we've joined these nice people. I know you won't succeed. But try."

"Don't hand me that shit, Lala."

"Come on, Billy. Cool it, man," Thomas said. It was almost a plea.

"Exactly who asked you your advice, Stepin Fetchit?"

I felt Kate's knee pressing against mine.

"You're also a lousy lay," Lala said. Out of the blue.

"Oh, well, well now. I'm sure I'm not as good as this spade here."

Jennifer arrived with the drinks, which was all we needed. Billy downed his double Irish whiskey in two gulps and took a long drink from his beer mug before she could remove the cork from the wine bottle. He rapped his empty shot glass on the tabletop. "Hit me again. Now."

"What in the name of God is eating you tonight?" I asked.

"He's jealous," Lala said.

"Me? Jealous?" Billy shouted indignantly.

"Because I spent so much time with Thomas at the court this afternoon when he was rallying with Helen and because I asked him to come along with us for dinner."

"Jealous! Now, that is the dumbest fucking thing I ever heard of in my life," Billy shouted.

"I could tell you about our house specials for this evening," Jennifer whispered.

"You just haul your ass and get me my whiskey. Move it."

Jennifer fled. People sitting at surrounding tables were glancing at us now.

Lala turned to us with a bright smile on her face. "Well, Mac and Kate, is it perfectly clear to both of you that Thomas and I once were lovers? Before I took up with this lard ass here? And I loved every minute of it."

"And for your added information, Mac and Kate, he also used to beat the hell out of her," Billy said.

"Kate and I could go," I said. "You three have things to talk about."

"I'm telling you, this one used to beat the living shit out of *this* one. Now, is that the truth or ain't it, Lala?"

"It only happened that once, Billy," Thomas said. "I thought you and me had worked it out."

"It was before Thomas broke his leg and the Bears would go to Washington to play the Redskins. That's how it started. Then when the season was over, Thomas used to go see her. By then she had run through every available man there in Washington, married or otherwise. Tell Mac that's the God's truth, Lala."

Lala didn't say anything, but she didn't have to.

"So she hides out in her own place for nearly a week using ice packs to bring the swelling down because she was ashamed to show her swollen face around town."

"Yes, it's true. Can't somebody find a way to shut him up?" Lala asked.

"Because if she had gone to lunch, say, at the Jockey Club, even wearing her big shades, somebody would be sure to spot her and say, Why, there's Lala Powers. But why is her fucking face so swollen and bruised? Even under them shades she's wearing, one can easily see her eyes are puffed up the size of grapefruit."

Jennifer brought his drink and placed it on the table before him as if she were setting a trap. Billy reached for it immediately.

"And somebody in the know, which was everybody in town, would say, Lala's face looks like an eggplant be-

141

cause that nigger football player from Chicago she's making it with beat the shit out of her."

"I forgot about it a long time ago," Lala said. "I started it and I deserved what I got."

Billy ignored her. "But you know, my dear, Lala must like it. Because one still sees the two of them chatting it up on the Cape."

Lala leaned forward and spoke softly. "Don't you just hate him? Isn't he the coarsest person you ever met?"

"And after Thomas and before me, there was Dolph, before he got remarried. Christ, everybody in the Washington metropolitan area, everybody on the entire Eastern seaboard knew about that one."

"That was legit," Lala said to Kate, leaving the rest of us out of it. "Dolph was between marriages. His first wife had been dead for about a year."

"I mean there was a time when perfect strangers would walk up to me in New York, I'm talking bums on the grates, and they would say, Is it true that Lala Powers and Dolph Bridges are having this big screw-out down in Washington? Because, this bum would say, this is what I myself am hearing on the fucking grapevine."

"Dolph and I were never anything to each other," Lala told Kate. "Just friends. Who screwed now and then, that's all. I was the one who introduced him to Helen, in fact."

"Yeah, go ahead, deny it, Lala. You slut," Billy said. "I'm telling you, I was hearing about it from bums on the street."

"Why do you put up with it?" Kate asked Lala, as if Billy weren't there.

Lala thought about it. "You know, I went to see a shrink about it. I asked him the same question, even though I know the answer. He's a different person when he's sober, is all I can say."

Jennifer was standing there, taking it all in, rocking in her Reeboks and trembling like a child who has just been ordered out of a cold pool on a cloudy day. She took a deep breath. "For an appetizer tonight we suggest the smoked bluefish?" She moaned. "Also we have, oh God, soup. I can't remember the name of the soup." She covered her face with her hands.

"I worked here as a waitress one summer, years ago," Kate said. "The first day on the job I spilled a whole entire bowl of clam chowder in a woman's lap." Red-limbed Jennifer smiled wanly.

"Chopped steak, rare. Fries," Billy said. "And another double neat. The drink now." The rest of us ordered the soup and the fish of the day.

I knew it was going to be a long time before the food arrived, three or four years. One of those nights. Billy kept ordering doubles. He appeared determined to drink himself into oblivion, but he was a beefy guy and a true boozer, so it took time. We became a silent table, waiting him out.

Jennifer served the soup. Billy's eyes rolled up and his head lolled back, then went forward slowly. His shoulders slumped and his head hit the tabletop with a dull thud. He moved no more.

Lala reached in his lap, got his napkin and draped it over his head. Jennifer took away the soup plates, brought the fish, something stuffed with crabmeat, and we ate while Billy snored softly. We canceled his chopped steak and I ordered another bottle of wine.

"I'll get him to the car," Thomas said.

"He's not disturbing us," I said.

"He will if he wakes. I'll sit with him there for a while. Better." Thomas hooked his hands under Billy's arms, gently got him to his feet, and led him away and out of the restaurant. Kate, Lala and I sat and drank the wine.

"You introduced Dolph to Helen," I said. "You must have known both of them from way back."

"I did. At a cocktail party somewhere. I'd known Helen since we were both married and in the same set. I knew Dolph from parties, dinners. There's a certain group of senators in Washington you know and a certain group you don't. Dolph was in the group you knew."

"How long did you live in Washington, Lala?" Kate asked.

"I got there in 1968."

"The year that was. The pits," I said.

"What was so bad about it?"

"You were just a kid then, Kate, so it went right by you. That was the year when everything seemed to go bad at once. The Tet offensive. King was killed. Bobby

Kennedy. The black riots in the cities. At the time it seemed like the whole damn country was coming apart at the seams."

"It blew right past me, too," Lala said. "I was pretty young, and new in Washington. I do remember the riot that spring when the Army troops were sent in. You couldn't leave the house for one entire weekend. Especially if you were living on Capitol Hill, which I was. And working for a House subcommittee."

"It must have been very exciting, working in Washington in those days," Kate said. Kate was captivated by her.

"Hell, I was young and unattached, a natural blonde with a body to die for, and I fucked like a mink. Any man I wanted I got. Mucho parties and upscale dates. Also, I was bright, damn it, bright. I wasn't *in* women's lib, I *was* women's lib. Before it had a name. Hell, I was Washington's golden girl for a couple of years, on everybody's A list for party invitations."

"God, it sounds exciting," Kate said. "I mean it sounds like something on television."

"You haven't heard it all. I married a rich man. Washington society. I made the social scene for a few years, on the right committees, blah, blah, blah."

"And screwed around a little on the side," I said. Kate glared at me. "From what I've heard," I added.

"I got divorced and, boy, do I wish I had that to do over again. It was a holy mess. I got caught having an affair. Washington society sided with my husband and dumped me. He let me have it with both barrels, right between the eyes, alimonywise. So I was left a social outcast, trying to make ends meet. I still am."

"That's a tough town," I said. "So you and Helen knew each other when you were both married. In the same set, you said. What was her first husband like?"

"Very social. Metropolitan Club, Chevy Chase Club. And not worth a damn."

"But charming."

"He could ride beautifully. And sail. He never worked a day in his life."

"A drinker?"

"No, that wasn't the problem. He was a social drinker, that's all. He wasn't rich. I said social, not rich. What he did was, he lived off other people's money. He lived off Helen's, what she had. You might say they lived off the land, her land."

"Helen was rich," I said. It wasn't a question.

"Old-time Washington society. Cliff dwellers they call themselves, except Helen's family is Virginia hunt country. Her father spent all the family money, so she inherited a farm and that was all. A beautiful farm, to be sure, but no money to keep it up, and an expensive husband to support. So she sold it off, acre by acre, to developers. That's what she and her first husband lived on. She and Dolph still live in the house, and there are barns. But the developers own all the land around. It's out in McLean."

"Then enter Dolph Bridges."

"He was made for her."

"You think she'd like being First Lady?"

"Absolutely to die for. Are you kidding? I know she says she hates politics. But she'd *love* being First Lady."

"Helen's the one that should be a made-for-television movie," Kate said. It sounded silly, but I knew better. Smart Kate was trying hard to draw Lala out for me, open her up, and she was succeeding very well.

"Social Washington hasn't had a First Lady since Jackie Kennedy," Lala said.

"You've lost me."

"Think of Washington as a small town, Kate, where everybody knows everybody else and where there's a very rigid social structure."

"As you found out the hard way," I said, which I shouldn't have.

"Up yours, Mac. Although you're right, I did. You've got to remember that most of the people who get elected president these days already live in Washington. People there know them, know their wives and children."

"Reagan and Carter didn't come from Washington."

"And Nancy Reagan and Rosalynn Carter never really were part of Washington society either. Nancy Reagan was L.A. glitz. Nobody in Washington really knew any of that crowd. Rosalynn Carter was a small-town Southern girl, strictly Georgia, a career Navy wife."

"Mrs. Johnson was a Washington woman," I said. "So were Pat Nixon and Betty Ford. All three of them raised families there, lived there for years. But you're saying none of them was part of the social Washington you're talking about."

"Lady Bird Johnson lived in northwest Washington. Both her daughters went to National Cathedral School. But the Johnsons' social life was strictly Texas Washington and Congress. Pat Nixon was Spring Valley until he was elected vice president. And Betty Ford was Arlington, Virginia, suburban split-level. Quaker Lane, just off Glebe Road, kids in the northern Virginia public schools."

"But Jackie was part of social Washington. It stays in place no matter who's president. Is that what you're telling us?" I asked.

"Absolutely. She lived there as a young single woman, remember, with her mother and her stepfather. Her half-sister still lives there. They're all part of the Georgetown set. The Chevy Chase set, the Metropolitan Club, Sulgrave Club set. They all go to the same private dances, to the Waltz Group. They all support the same charities, the Opera Ball, the Symphony Ball, the Corcoran Ball. They entertain each other, their children all go to the same private schools, National Cathedral, Saint Alban's, Landon. Hell, they even go to the same churches."

"It is a group in which I presume Dolph and Helen are members in good standing?"

"Dolph slowly became part of it. Helen always was, was born to it."

"Even poor, as a penniless widow?"

"Somebody always had an extra ticket, an extra seat at the table they had paid for at the ball. She was invited to all the parties. Yes, she always was part of it, in the Green Book. That's the Washington social register."

"So if Dolph gets elected—"

"Helen would be queen of the Potomac. She would rule the place, decide who's in and who's out. Where you buy your clothes. Who does your hair. Where you eat lunch. The list is endless."

"Would she like that? She told me this morning it doesn't matter to her one way or the other."

"Are you kidding? You have got to be kidding. You understand what it is I'm saying? I don't think Helen cares very much one way or another about being First Lady of the nation. I think she would love to be social queen of Washington."

"You're saying she would glory in it, would love it."

"To die for," Lala said.

12

SOMETIMES KATE ATTENDED SUNDAY morning mass and sometimes she didn't, according to her mood. It all seemed to depend on whether she woke up loving and needing God more than she hated the Church. The following morning she did go, slipped out of bed without waking me and made the nine o'clock at St. John's. Kate liked and trusted Father Riley more than she would admit.

I had breakfast laid out when she returned shortly after ten, and we ate on the patio, scrambled cheese eggs, English muffins, fresh orange juice that I had squeezed, coffee and Mrs. Adams's wild beach plum jelly, the heavenly concoction of a local woman who looked like Aunt Bea in the Andy Griffith show and who owned and operated a little jam and jelly business out of her home. There was no mention of any diet, maybe because it was a Sunday.

Kate had stopped at the Alden variety store and

bought the Sunday papers, New York, Boston, Hyannis, and we had another Cape Cod morning to share. I thought nothing could be more pleasant, a sun-dappled patio on a quiet Sunday morning in June, a full stomach, a pot of hot coffee within reach, a big stack of fresh newspapers to read, and a good-looking woman you loved sitting across from you with her feet in your lap, occasionally wiggling her toes in your crotch, looking at you briefly as if to say she was thinking seriously about it. I'll take it, take out a loan or pay for it on time if I have to. Wrap it up and put my name on it. Let other men go out and hit golf balls.

"Bascombe's coming over," she told me around noon. "We've got a mountain of trust stuff to go over."

"I've got lots of work to do myself. I've got to start shaping that article on Dolph Bridges sooner or later."

"Is Billy that way all the time? I know he's an old friend of yours."

"I think something's on his mind."

"Whatever it is, he drinks too much."

"He's also crazy about Lala Powers, and he's jealous."

"He made it to mass and confession this morning, looking awful."

"I'll bet. What did he have to say?"

"I don't think he saw me. Or if he did, he didn't want to talk. He certainly didn't strike me last night as a religious type, but there he was this morning, on his knees."

"Billy told me once that when he was a kid he seriously thought about becoming a priest."

"The Church has more than enough like him already, thank you."

I stood up. "I'll leave you to Bascombe. I've got to get going."

"Out?"

"I've got a hunch Billy Nolan talked to Father Riley."

"It's not quite noon. Bascombe's not arriving until one. We could take a few minutes." She wiggled her toes in my lap.

Terry Riley declined when I telephoned and offered to buy him lunch. "There's nothing edible in North Walpole. I'm cooking. Why don't you come over here? There's plenty. Kate, too, of course, if she'd like. I was thrilled and pleased to see that beautiful face of hers at the nine o'clock this morning."

"Thanks, but she's got trust business with Bascombe. I'm on my way, however."

"I'll have a bloody waiting for you."

He did, too, had it in his hand when he opened the front door at St. John's rectory. His older brother Dennis was a wholesale liquor dealer in South Boston and there was always plenty of booze in the house.

We sat in the kitchen, which was one of Riley's major places to be in life, along with the church altar and the outdoor basketball court at St. John's High School next door, where, every afternoon, he joined in the after-school pickup game. There was an office in the rectory, of course, with a library, but Terry wasn't much for reading. He spent his time at his desk, doing his paperwork, but he was not an office man. Terry Riley was a kitchen man.

He was a superb cook, and complained at times when things were not going well that he had chosen the wrong career. I finished the bloody Mary and we sat at the big wooden kitchen table and had bowls of spicy gazpacho, which he brought from the refrigerator, and drank a crisp white French table wine sent down by his brother. The Red Sox were playing the Yankees and we watched it on a little color Sony.

"I thought poor parish priests were supposed to have small black-and-whites at best," I said.

"A little present. Last week. From Dody Munro, bless her."

"Charls Munro's wife? I've met him, not her."

"A pleasant woman."

"And a thoughtful one."

"She's always giving me little things, nice things, when she sees the need, or comes across the things. Her family's from around here, you know. She was born and raised down in Falmouth. A good Irish Catholic, as they say. Worried to death about her boy, she is. My son the hippie, she calls him. I guess he's given them trouble since he was fourteen or so." He got up, walked over to the refrigerator and looked inside. "Paulette Murphy dragged Rocko to mass this morning, and good for her because Rocko takes some dragging after one of his Saturday nights at the Binnacle."

"I wish I'd been here to see it." Rocko Murphy was a commercial fisherman, a guy I had got in a fight with shortly after I arrived in North Walpole back in January. A little misunderstanding had caused him to punch me out and throw me through a plate-glass window at the Binnacle.

"He brought me a little scrod," Terry said. "Fresh off his boat and filleted with his own hands." He put a big black frying pan on the stove, dumped in a lump of sweet butter and turned on the gas flame. Then he quickly mixed flour with curry powder, about three parts to one, coated the pieces of fish and, when the butter was hot, sautéed them.

"I'm not wild about cod of any size," he said as we ate. "Lacks taste. But it's inexpensive and the curry helps. I've got some sour cream raisin pie for after. Big guys like us need a little volume in a meal."

I nodded my head in agreement while I ate. Who was I to argue with a man of God? We drank coffee with the pie and watched the ball game.

"I've been working hard, for a change," I told him. "A profile on Senator Dolph Bridges for the *New York Times*. And I've been stringing for the *Globe* on that drowning at Cranberry House. You know the one I mean. The young woman in the yellow VW. Susan Jacobs was her name. Only twenty-six. A young Washington office worker. You must have read about it."

The priest took a beat just as Jim Rice of the Red Sox took a first called strike. "Oh, yes. Yes, of course, I've read about it. Noah's been investigating it, I assume."

"He's been looking into it. I don't think he's come up with much of anything. In fact, it's my guess he's about to close the case and declare the death an accidental drowning. Even though her body was found in the passenger's seat of the car. With her seat belt on." Rice fouled back.

"Is that a fact?" He pointed with his fork at my plate. "More? Half? Otherwise, it'll go to waste."

"Well, I usually say no to sweets."

"Bullshit!" Riley shouted. Like any good cook, he liked people to eat his food. He got up and cut the pie.

"Noah had a strong notion at first that the girl had been murdered," I said. "That, or accidental homicide." Jim Rice hit a double, which rebounded off the left-field wall in Fenway Park, and went into second standing up.

"He still doesn't hold that belief?" Don Baylor was at bat.

"He can't come up with anything, not so far." Baylor took two straight balls, fouled to left, then a third.

"Should he do that quite yet, close the investigation? Sometimes it takes time for the dust to settle, before people start coming forward."

"Nobody's come forward so far," I said, and after a long pause added, "Unless you know something I don't." Baylor walked and Evans hit a single into right on the first pitch. Rice came around to score and Baylor slid into third.

"How's the article on Senator Bridges coming along?" Terry Riley asked.

"Okay. I'm lucky. A friend of mine is on the staff, guy named Billy Nolan." Rich Gedman was up, taking practice swings at the plate as if he intended to try to hit the ball somewhere into New Hampshire.

"You know, maybe you'd know him if you saw him," I said. "He's Catholic. Big beer gut, black curly hair and blue eyes, black Irish with a New York accent. I know he's been to mass and confession here a few times."

"Oh, hell, there are so many. And sometimes, to tell the truth, unless it's something big, my mind's on other things."

A swing and a miss by Gedman.

"Talking about Susan Jacobs, the young woman Noah thinks probably was murdered, it turns out she worked in Washington on a subcommittee Bridges used to chair. A coincidence, as far as anybody can tell. They didn't even know she was up here."

"Is that a fact?"

"And there she was, living in the waitress dorm at Cranberry House, right across the Cut from the Munro house, not two hundred yards away."

156

The priest stretched out his legs, placed his hands behind his head, and we watched the game for a while. Gedman flied out, or should have. The ball dropped between the shortstop and the center fielder. Baylor tagged up and scored.

"You don't think Noah should give up on his investigation, do you?" I asked.

"No, I don't. I think he should ask around some more. Understand, I know little or nothing about police work."

Henderson flied out, ending the inning. Terry Riley, straddling a seesaw between church and state, between his vows and his view of justice, had told me all he could. I would have bet money that Billy had confessed to him. Confessed what? On the tube, Mickey Spillane and Rodney Dangerfield were busy selling Miller Lite.

I gassed up the boat at the Pilgrim Harbor marine dock, signed the charge slip, then made my way slowly through the harbor, out to the Cut, carefully obeying the *No Wake* signs along the way. Empty in winter, except for a few rusty commercial fishing boats, the harbor now was filled with pleasure craft of every description, day-sailers, catboats, powerboats, motor-sailers, sleek sloops, fat comfortable yawls and ketches. I liked to read their names as I rode past them, *Daddy's Mink*, *At Last*, *Exactement*, *Non Sequitur*.

The fourteen-foot Boston Whaler I was in had a forty-horsepower Mercury outboard engine. The boat had come with the house left to Kate. I found the fiberglass hull upside down on a frame in the yard, the engine on a mount in the garage. I had used it a lot that spring.

I liked to cruise around the harbor with Kate on a nice afternoon with a bottle of wine and a portable radio, liked to take it through the Cut into Nantucket Sound early in the morning to fish for breakfast flounder, and liked to go out alone now and then, full-speed the throttle, and give my frustrations a good blowout.

Billy Nolan was waiting for me on the Munro dock, blue-and-white Playmate at his side. It was five in the afternoon on one of the longest days in the year, so the sun was still high.

I pulled alongside the dock and idled the motor. He got in, sat down, and I pulled away, heading through the Cut, into the sound. "Like I told you on the phone, I thought a little fresh salt air might do us both a world of good," I said.

"Sorry about last night."

"Women can do that to you. Also, you drink too much. You can't handle it anymore, Billy."

He opened the Playmate, popped two cans of Bud and handed one to me. "See, this is what other people also have told me."

"Is Lala still speaking to you?"

"This I don't know. She left for the city this morning before I got up. Nonstop Hyannis to La Guardia."

Billy was wearing gray K-Mart cotton trousers, a white

dress shirt with the sleeves rolled up and black wingtip shoes, a brown-whiskey man in white-wine country.

I opened up the throttle on the Whaler as soon as we passed through the Cut, the bow rose, and we were off on a twenty-knot ride in the sound, bucking and bounding as we crisscrossed the wakes of the larger boats. Salt spray flew back from the bow, wetting and stinging our faces. Billy hung in there, popped another Bud.

We zoomed around in the sound for fifteen minutes or so, then I throttled down and we went back through the Cut, passing the Munro house on our left hand and Cranberry House restaurant on our right, entering Pilgrim Harbor. Billy opened the Playmate again and pulled out a pint of Canadian Club this time, drank from the bottle, chased it with his beer and shuddered. He offered the bottle to me but I held up my hand.

Noah Simmons was waiting inside the harbor as he and I had agreed in our telephone conversation after I left Terry Riley's rectory. He was sprawled on the bow of one of his police boats, wearing swim trunks, flippers and a scuba-diving mask, which he had pushed up on top of his head. "Hey, Noah!" I called and stopped the boat. He waved in salute, adjusted his mask over his face, flopped into the water like a huge sea lion, swam casually over and draped his big arms over the side of the Whaler. I nodded toward the police boat. "What's going on?"

"Nothing unusual. It's the beginning of the summer season and we like to put on a show of force for the tourists, convince them we mean business. We try to show them we have the men and the boats to enforce our summer harbor rules. Which we don't, of course. We'd have to double taxes in this town."

Noah crawled on board. I introduced him to Billy and Billy helped himself to a big gurgle from the Canadian Club bottle and didn't bother to chase it. "I'm a native New Yorker, okay?"

Neither of us said anything. After all, we were there only on my hunch, that and a couple of unconnected facts.

"So you two got me floating around out here," Billy said.

"Noah and I want to talk to you, Billy. That's all," I said.

"I don't want to. Look at this big bastard. You think I don't know muscle when I see it?" He crushed the beer can and threw it in the water, breaking one of Noah's firmest beach rules. "Get me the fuck back to the house."

"Billy, something's troubling you. You're holding back, not telling all you know. Did anybody up here with Bridges know Susan Jacobs was in town?"

"Mac, we are talking about a lot being at stake here."

"We are talking about obstruction of justice, possibly. Also possibly we are talking about murder."

"We are talking about innocent people who became victims of circumstance."

"It's all going to come out sooner or later, Billy."

"What are you talking about?"

"You're all trying to protect Dolph Bridges. Something happened the night Susan Jacobs died. What? What happened?"

We glared at each other. Noah was watching silently.

"Thou shalt not lie or bear false witness. It's in the Bible. You can look it up," I told him.

"Christ," Billy said, wearily, sadly, almost to himself. "Okay, she was over there, over to the house that night. So what does that prove?"

Noah and I looked at each other. Big news. "Why?" I asked.

"That I don't know. We were having an outdoor steak fry, celebrating an endorsement that meant a lot to us. She just showed up." Breathing heavily, Billy was, as if he had run a long race and was getting his breath back.

"Give us a nice ride around the harbor, Mac," Noah said. "Maybe go up Clam Pond." I knew he was excited but he kept it out of his voice.

I took us under the bridge, the same bridge I had driven over in panic the morning I spotted Susan Jacobs's car in the water. This afternoon we waved up at the kids who were flounder-fishing along the railings. A narrow, winding channel, and not a very deep one even at high tide, led from the harbor to the salt pond, and I made my way through it slowly, obeying all the markers.

Noah was in the bow of the boat, lying back on a couple of life preservers and facing Billy, who sat amidships, legs spread. Billy tossed him a beer and Noah caught it, popped it. "You said a steak fry."

"You know, an outdoor cookout with a charcoal grill, New York cuts, baked potato in foil, salad. Out on the patio."

"So it was a party, then?"

"You could call it that. You know this senator named Lifsey from Alabama? This old bastard has been there since they wore striped pants and morning coats almost."

"Lifsey's the first long-term Republican senator from the South since Reconstruction," I said to Noah. "He's got lots of power and influence with other Southern Republicans."

"Dolph's been stroking him for years. Hell, he even flew down there for his daughter-in-law's funeral. They got to be big asshole buddies on the Appropriations Committee. The old man promised he would endorse Dolph eventually. This spring, early, he begins to get wishy-washy about it."

"And all of you started to get worried."

"We thought he might decide to come out for nobody, just stay out of it. He's eighty-one and he's planning to run for reelection himself. If you can imagine that."

"He'll win, too," I said. "The only way to get him out will be to drive a silver stake through his heart. He wanted something from you. What did it cost you to bring him around?"

162

Billy shrugged. "Not a lot. Dolph had to promise to back him for chairman of the platform committee at the convention."

"Hoo, boy."

"So who are you? The president of Common Cause? You get in this business seriously, some things you got to do. You know that."

"He'll deliver Dolph a platform Warren Harding couldn't run on."

"He will help bring other Southern Republicans around, you dumb shit. Thurmond. Helms. The younger ones. That's the important thing. All he wants is the chance to shoot off his mouth at the convention, make the nightly news. A small price to pay. Who's the last candidate to pay any attention to a party platform?"

"So there was good cause for celebration," Noah said. "Who was there?"

"Dolph and Helen, Thomas Duncan, Eliot More and me. Plus the guy who owns the house. Charls Munro."

"He's Dolph Bridges's national finance chairman," I told Noah.

"I know of him. A guy owns property like that, I know about him."

"And Munro's wife, she was there. A stout lady, like me, and middle-aged."

"Her name's Dody," I said. "She was born somewhere on the Cape. Munro operates out of Chicago. He's a corporate takeover artist who's savaged at least half a dozen companies."

"Sometimes you need people like that," Billy said. "That's the way it is in politics."

"Munro's a bloodsucker, Billy. He needs a dozen lawyers on his payroll all the time. You look at the companies he's taken over, the careers he's ruined, the divorces, the suicides he's caused, all in the name of increased stockholder profits and efficiency, he's a greedy bloodsucker."

"Just the seven of you? You said Miss Jacobs was there," Noah said.

"Showed up. The party was nothing fancy. All in the family, you might say. Everybody was up. Even Thomas, who brought the fucking house down with his imitation of Lifsey." Billy sucked on his beer, pulled a cigar out of his pocket, lit it and spat in the water. Noah's water, I thought, although Noah seemed to pay the move no notice.

"What do you mean, 'showed up'? She wasn't invited?"

"I thought she was at first, as somebody's guest. Lots of times we have people around, you know."

"So you'd never seen her before."

"None of us had, as it turned out. See, we all went to work for Dolph *after* he left the Senate. I'll say it. We're all hired guns. We didn't know her, and she comes wandering out on the patio barefoot, half naked, in a sort of wraparound skirt and a strapless bra that was barely covering her boobs."

The clothes she was wearing when I pulled her body out of her car. "She must have made quite an impression," I said.

"It was dark. We had four or five of them kerosene tropical torches, like Don the Beachcomber, you know? Dolph and Helen were off to the far side of the patio, chatting it up with this Munro and his wife, which should lose weight, you ask me."

Noah had closed his eyes. I knew he was trying to place himself on that patio, among that group. I kept the Whaler headed up Clam Pond, meandering lazily around the tilted channel markers. Summer was replacing spring on the Cape as subtly as a cloudy-day sunrise. Along the shore, smoke was drifting up from the lawns, summer people, early arrivers, grilling burgers on their Webers. The pond was alive. God, I loved it.

"She walks over to me like she knows me. I was standing with Thomas and Eliot. She says to me, 'Hello, sailor. Buy a girl a drink?' Which, still thinking she was a guest of some sort, I decided to display good manners. Which I can, despite what Mac here might have told you."

"Called upon, inspired, challenged, Billy can bring to mind David Niven," I said.

"What did you say to her?"

"I told her she looked like Venus rising from the waves. Which she did, sort of. And I asked her what I might get for her to drink. To which she said a glass of vodka with a little grapefruit juice on the side."

"Was she drunk?"

"I think about it now, I think she was high. Euphoric. Like she'd had a big snort of coke, acted like it."

"You've seen people on cocaine?"

"I'm from New York, remember."

"Did she have anything to say to anybody else? She sounds like she was on a roll. Anything to say to Thomas Duncan, for example?"

"She punched him in the rib cage. 'Big brown dude. How's it going with you?' she said."

"Did she know Thomas Duncan?"

"That's when I went to get the drink."

"But when you left, they were talking. Chatting?"

"I guess. I don't remember. I'd had a few beers myself."

"I've been wondering about Thomas. How did he get so close to Dolph Bridges? Through you?" I asked.

"Wrong, totally wrong. They met at one of these pro-celebrity tennis tournaments. Thomas and Helen were both playing in it. Dolph figured he needed black identification, which being an Illinois Republican he never bothered to promote."

"And what better way to get it than to be seen with Thomas Duncan," I said.

"Mac, you got it. And here I was thinking what a dumb shit you are. Except they really got tight. Thomas became almost like a member of the family. Remember,

Thomas's career was on the way down when they met. He worships the ground Dolph walks on, do anything for him."

"What happened after you brought Susan Jacobs her vodka?" Noah asked, a bulldozer, a tank, in his questioning. He would not allow any long divergence from the narrative of what happened at dinner that night.

"She drank it. What do you think?" Billy said. "Slug of vodka, sip of grapefruit juice."

"Think about this before you answer. Did she appear to you to have been under the influence of anything other than coke and booze?"

"Drugs? Pills, you mean? Maybe. The subject never came up. But she was hyper, euphoric, like I said. On a roll, as you put it. Except she said 'tracing around.' Two or three times. Tracing around. Who can keep up with kid talk?"

"Did she stay for dinner?"

"No. She, well, staggers out after two drinks, without a word to anybody. I thought she'd gone to the head."

"She never talked to Senator Bridges or his wife?"

"No. Let me think. No. She did ask if any jobs would be coming open in New Hampshire. Eliot told her to call her the next day and they'd talk about it."

Noah sighed. "Not much to go on, is there? A drunk girl looking for a campaign job."

"See. I've been trying to tell you two that there's nothing there."

We were down at the eastern end of Clam Pond. To

the right I could see the house where Kate and I lived. Bascombe Midgeley's new Pontiac station wagon was parked in the driveway. Bascombe traded for a new car every year, a dealer's dream man.

Noah pulled on his flippers and offered Billy his hand. "It's been nice meeting you. And thanks for your help. I'm simply trying to wrap this thing up."

"Sure. I can understand that. Glad to be of help."

Noah rolled off the Whaler, into the water. *"Te posterius videbo*, alligator," he said to me. "I'll swim back, check out the channel underwater."

I turned the boat, headed back down Clam Pond, under the bridge again, and through Pilgrim Harbor to the Munro dock.

"I don't mind telling you, I'm glad to get that cleared up," Billy said.

"I think there's more to it than you told Noah, Billy."

Billy opened his mouth in astonishment. "What is this I am hearing here?" We pulled up to the dock but Billy didn't move from his seat in the boat.

"Come on," I said.

"Mac, you don't know how this thing has been bothering me. I even made confession and mass this morning."

"Tell me the parts you left out."

"When she starts to leave, tracing out, she called it, she suddenly says she'll just say hello to her old boss. And before any of us could stop her, she staggers over to him, kisses him on both cheeks, gives him a hug and starts whispering sweet nothings in his ear. Thomas and I go over to pull her away. She shakes Helen's hand, introduces herself and tells her what a wonderful president Dolph is going to make. Munro and his wife are standing there, looking at her. She introduces herself to them."

"And everything was hanging out, you said."

"Right out of *Playboy*. Tits and legs flying in all directions. She has one hand on Dolph's shoulder to keep from falling, telling him she wants him to know he'll get nothing but full cooperation and support from her."

"Dolph must have been glad she took the time to drop by and assure him of that."

"She said something about he didn't have to worry that she would go around shooting her mouth off."

"It turned out she was right about that. Anything else?"

"Maybe they'd see each other around, she tells him." Billy Nolan hurled his empty beer can into the water. "Christ, it's going to blow up in our faces," he said. "I always knew it would."

13

I DIDN'T TELL NOAH. I decided to look around myself before I told him. Duty would have compelled Noah to begin an official investigation. Word would have gotten out. News like that is too hot and viscous, especially in a presidential election year.

It would have become another national media riot. There would be an inquest, requested by the district attorney and ordered by the district court, and that would draw hundreds of reporters and photographers. The Cape's skies would be filled with chartered fixed-wing aircraft and helicopters flying videotapes to Boston, Providence and New York; parking lots around the district courthouse in Barnstable would be filled with tape-editing vans and transmission satellite trucks. The courthouse would be a madhouse, with dozens of hot video-news kids, young, good-looking and frantic to make the big career breakthrough from local to net they would tell grandchildren about one day, not to mention my pencil brothers, desperate to find one new fact no other print reporter had come up with. The story, what people would have bet a million dollars happened, would be the talk of the town.

And even if innocent, Dolph Bridges would see his presidential hopes dashed in the process. Let us salute the power of the press and bow before it. I decided to give Dolph the benefit of the doubt. Damned if I would be responsible for holding the match to the fuse of the bomb. It's called playing God.

So I didn't tell Noah.

I should have told Noah.

Instead, I called David Terrell, my editor at the *Times Magazine*, and asked him to authorize expenses for a trip to Washington to interview some of Dolph Bridges's former associates in the Senate and to take a closer look at his political action committee, which is the boiler room, the main power plant, of any modern presidential campaign. He quickly agreed. I didn't tell him anything about Susan Jacobs's death.

Kate and I got up early the next morning and drove to Boston, along Route 6 and across the Sagamore bridge. Even on an early Monday morning the oncoming traffic was heavy, lots of loaded station wagons, lots of cars towing pleasure boats. The Cape was filling up fast.

We parted company with a kiss in Boston, Kate and I. She was flying to Chicago to rendezvous with Martha Jacobs, Susan's sister, for the funeral. My offer to go along had been turned down cold. It was to be just the two of them, old college roommates who had shared four close years of study and gossip and growth and had remained friends ever since.

"It's what Martha wants," Kate told me as we made our way slowly through the early morning commuter rush-hour traffic, up I-93 bumper to bumper, on our way to Logan Airport. "There are no other members of the immediate family and she didn't want any of her parents' friends to come. So it's just the two of us."

"She changed her mind about cremation, obviously."

"That was frustration and despair speaking out, Mac. We've arranged a little graveside service. Susie's being buried beside her parents."

"That's good. Goddamn this traffic. Excuse me."

"It's getting worse every year. They're Reform Jews, and the rabbi who buried her parents and gave Martha and Susan their bat mitzvahs is going to be there, oh, to read the Twenty-third Psalm and say some prayers."

I didn't tell Kate either, didn't tell her that wild little Susie, tracing around, letting it all hang out, or most of it, had kissed Dolph Bridges and told him not to worry, that he could count on her to keep her mouth shut. I didn't tell her because I knew she and Martha had a tough enough day ahead of them as it was.

We both flew Delta.

Your nation's capital is a town of many interconnecting societies—federal Washington, military Washington, diplomatic Washington, business Washington—and within these are large and important secondary subsocieties. Congressional Washington is one.

The thin but strong cord that holds them all together like fish on a string is gossip. A young congressman from North Jesus gets caught with his pants down one night, they are talking about it at coffee break on the Hill the next morning, and an hour and one phone call later, they are laughing about it over a brown-bag lunch at the Bureau of Standards.

Towns gossip; industries, professions gossip. Only in Washington it very often ends up in the newspapers, on the nightly news. What crackerjack reporters there do is take it all in, encourage it, pass it along, take notes, try to separate fact from rumor and, too often, say *To hell with it* and write the rumor, heard often enough, with lots of *Officials speculated privately* and *Knowledgeable sources said* thrown in. That's called news analysis.

From Washington National Airport I took a cab straight to Capitol Hill, to the Dirksen office building. The driver was a very old black man, a private owner, self-employed, who drove an old Chrysler Imperial. "Get out of my way," he kept shouting at the young Puerto Rican and Iranian drivers we passed on the way. "Foreign assholes trying to take bread out of our mouths."

Spring had left the city behind and summer was settling in for a long stay. The trees were fully leaved and it showed promise of being a hot and humid day.

I was on a hunting expedition, prepared and anxious to shoot at anything that came in sight. From a pay phone in the main Senate cafeteria I called the staff director of the Senate Foreign Relations Committee, explained my mission, and he said he could give me a half hour. Dirksen 439, I could come right up.

Davis Putney, in his forties, combed his black hair straight back. Add to that a powder blue plaid suit, a baby blue broadcloth shirt, a solid navy blue necktie and, at first glance, he reminded you of that assistant high school principal whose guts you hated so much. The diploma on his office wall informed you that you were dealing with a Johns Hopkins Ph.D. in international relations. Of course, his opening words to me were "I have a meeting I've got to make at eleven." Every Davis Putney in this world I know has a meeting at eleven.

"This is for a major profile in the *Times Magazine*," I told him.

He nodded and began to pack a pipe, choosing one from many held in a rack on his desktop. It was an ornate pipe rack, which looked as if he had bought it in some sweaty African airport, using the last of his local currency at the end of a junket. He lit the pipe, sending fruity, nutty streams of smoke out both ends of his mouth. "We're both pros. Ask your questions," he said.

"I'm interested in your professional evaluation of Dolph Bridges. His competence as you witnessed it on the committee. Was he lazy? Did he do his homework? Is he really interested in foreign affairs?"

Davis Putney contemplated the question, puffing away. The smoke coming out of his mouth was enough to have been the beginning of a major mosquito-eradication program in the Louisiana swamps. "Dolph is tops. Absolutely," he said. "No Fulbright, mind you, but informed, involved, curious, ever questioning. He would have made a fine full-committee chairman. And you may quote me on that one, my friend."

"What about as president?"

"I think he would be the sort who is very actively involved in foreign affairs, but who would want a strong, competent secretary of state."

"You sound pretty high on him."

"Off the record completely, some of the people who drift off and on this committee over the years are ignorant nuts who couldn't identify the continents if you asked them. Senator Bridges is a sophisticated man."

Davis Putney was chumming the waters, of course, because there was a big fish out there and anything could happen if he hooked it and played it right, a job on the White House national security staff, a highly visible spot as an assistant secretary of state. Black-tie embassy dinners. Luxury travel with the secretary of state—hell, when the trip was to the right part of the world, in Air Force One with the president himself. A limo to pick you up at home every morning and take you home at night— power, intrigue and glitter. All that was possible.

"I know foreign affairs is a tricky, complicated business that takes experts. So I'm sure Senator Bridges has been calling on you more and more for your advice," I said.

"We keep in touch. Let's leave it at that."

"Researching this profile, I've noticed Dolph doesn't have a foreign policy adviser on his campaign staff. But hanging around as I've been doing, I keep hearing your name pop up. Davis thinks this. Or, I know Davis Putney believes that. This is what I'm hearing, so don't be surprised if you get a very important phone call one day soon."

Old Putney was puffing on his pipe furiously. I thought his eyes were going to pop out of his head. "As I say, we do keep in close touch."

"Do you mind if I say in my profile in the *Times* that among others he consults on foreign affairs is Davis Putney? With your title and so forth? 'Seems to value Putney's advice.' Something like that?"

"I wouldn't want to be listed as a *major* figure. But as someone providing input, I don't see any harm in that."

"You know, I think I'm getting too close to this story. That can happen. You begin to feel as if you're on the team. It's a danger in my business."

A sparrow was perched on a tree limb outside Putney's office window. The bird was peering at me, head cocked to one side.

"I only hope the story of Susan Jacobs's accident doesn't get out of hand," I said. "What an unfortunate coincidence that she worked on the staff of Dolph's old subcommittee. People make so much out of things, especially in a presidential election year." The sparrow winked at me.

"Hmm," Putney said. I thought he was going to swallow his pipe.

"Like Jimmy Carter saying in *Playboy* magazine that he had lust in his heart. As if these people weren't human beings, after all."

It worked. Davis Putney had the harassed look of a worried man, the look of a man who, thirty miles down the road, concludes that he probably has taken a wrong turn. He was glancing about, out his office window at the bird, at the autographed pictures on his walls, at his closed office door, as if he were looking for help. Had him. Except I didn't know what I had caught.

"Has the story come out down here?" I asked. "Anything in the locals? Any inquiries about her from the *Post*, or the news magazines? Anything like that?"

"No. Nothing," he managed to say.

"Good. Of course, the story is of considerably more interest to readers in New England. Chappaquiddick and all. I know because I also work part time for the Boston *Globe* and I'm their reporter on this one, too, I'm afraid."

"What does that mean?" The staff man would never make a diplomat, never in a million years.

"It means I'm caught out on a limb on this one. This *Globe* editor I've got is a tough old Irishman, a *Front Page* type you might say. The Jacobs girl did die under somewhat mysterious circumstances and he wants a feature story from me about her, a takeout on her life-style and so forth."

"Surely he's not trying to tie the Senator to her death?"

"Davis, you know Washington's reputation out in the hinterlands, which is Sin City. The typist on the congressional payroll who can't type but does other things very well, if you know what I mean. The congressman and his wife who fornicate at night on the very steps of the Capitol. Fanny Foxe in the Tidal Basin. Out in the hinterlands they think stuff like that goes on all the time. At least this editor in Boston does. You ought to hear him go on about it."

"Have you talked to Senator Bridges about this story assignment?"

"So far I've referred to Miss Jacobs in print only as a federal office worker from Washington," I said. "Dolph is worried about it. But, of course, you must know that. You must have been in contact with North Walpole on this."

"Well. I wouldn't want to comment on that."

"Did you tell the other staff members on the committee? They must have wondered what happened to her, leaving so suddenly. Did you post a memo or something? Maybe their reaction is something I can use to satisfy my editor and get him off my back."

"You'd be wasting your time talking to them, I'm afraid. Susan was well liked, but she didn't have close friends on the staff. They'd all tell you they remember her as a good worker and a cheerful person, that's all."

"She wasn't a hell raiser? This editor of mine has the idea she was a little wild."

"That's the Washington myth you were talking about, Mac."

"I'll tell my editor that." I clapped my hands in relief.

It was better than nothing. I left his office convinced that he had been working closely with Dolph and his staff to keep a lid on this. I had known they were worried. Now, I realized, they were scared. And I would have bet big money that Davis Putney was already on the phone to North Walpole.

If you like to look at pretty girls in summer dresses, Judiciary Square at high noon on a sunny day in early June is one of the best places in the world to do it. The little park, just across the street from the old Senate office building, has a lush lawn, lots of benches and a grove of hardwood trees that provide good shade. Young women who work at the Capitol go there with brown-bag lunches to eat, gossip, tan their legs and get a breath of fresh air.

I hung around in the hallway outside the Foreign Relations Committee offices for a few minutes after Davis Putney and I parted company. It was lunchtime. I waited until I spotted two young women about the age of Susan Jacobs who walked out of the office carrying lunch bags.

I followed them down the elevator, out of the office building and down Constitution Avenue to the park, waited until they picked a spot on the grass, then approached them. Pretty as a picture, both of them were.

"Excuse me," I said. "You see, I'm almost positive you're the people I'm looking for. But I've forgotten your names."

They glanced at each other knowingly, then glared at me. "I beg your pardon?" the redhead said.

"I've just come from the Foreign Relations Committee office. You do work there, don't you? Otherwise I've made a terrible mistake. They gave me your names and description and told me you'd be here in the park. But I'm bad on names. Did you know Susan Jacobs? Davis Putney told me you did."

They relaxed when they heard the names. I wasn't an old guy making a pass. "Yes. We both knew Susan," the redhead said. "Who are you?"

"My name's McFarland and I'm a newspaper reporter up in Boston. I'm doing a story on Miss Jacobs's tragic accident."

"Mr. Putney posted a memo about it. I'm Margy Bennifer and this is Carol Steeves. What do you want to know about Susie?"

I sat down on the grass beside them. "The summer tourists are arriving on the Cape now, hordes of them, and my paper thinks an article about her accident might serve as a warning to other people."

"You mean about not going out in small boats alone, especially if you're not experienced?"

"Something like that."

"Mr. Putney told us about it in his memo. Poor Susie. And to think it happened there in Hyannisport, where all the Kennedys live."

"Yes. It's very sad. Did you two know Susan very well?"

"We were friends," Carol Steeves said. "We talked a lot in the office, you know? And we had lunch together lots of times. But we were never close after work. Wouldn't you say, Margy?"

"What kind of girl was she? We don't know much about her except, like Mr. Putney wrote in his memo, that she died in a small boating accident in Hyannisport."

"Susie was real wacky. Wouldn't you say, Margy?"

"From another world," Margy the redhead said.

"She was sort of a mystery to us. Wouldn't you say, Margy?"

"Some mornings she would come in, I'd swear she hadn't been to bed. At least, not to sleep. Excuse me, but we're all adults."

"From what you two say, she sounds exactly like the sort of person who would get out in a small boat in Hyannisport and get herself in trouble."

"She would do anything and say anything. You never

knew what she was going to say or do next. Margy? I mean, well, wouldn't you say?"

"Did she have any sort of special relationship with Senator Bridges? Something funny? Like a standing joke between them? Something I could use as an anecdote? Readers love things like that."

They looked at each other.

"What would you say, Margy?" Carol asked.

"If you don't want me to use the name, I could say one of the senators she worked for. Or a senator on the subcommittee she worked for. Something like that."

"Margy, what about the party at his house last summer?" Carol asked.

"You quote us on this and we'll both lose our jobs," Margy said to me. "Davis Putney is one mean shit."

"I'll write, a person who observed the incident, or who was there."

"Last summer he was floor manager of the trade bill, and when it passed he gave a big Saturday-afternoon party at his house out in Virginia to celebrate. Hamburgers and beer, softball, swimming. It was a lot of fun."

"And about three in the afternoon, Susie arrives with her boyfriend, on his motorcycle. A real hog, I remember she called it," Carol said. "They came riding up on the lawn with *her* driving. We all laughed about that. Remember, Margy?"

"Who was her boyfriend? Do you remember his name by any chance?"

"Who could forget it? Randall Randall. A marine stationed down at Quantico. A shaved head, except he was sporting a long black wig."

"Lots of enlisted kids from Quantico do that on weekends," Carol said. "Because I used to go out last year with a guy stationed down there, a lieutenant, I mean. He told me that, which is perfectly understandable, Margy. Because they don't like going in Georgetown bars and have the other kids make fun of them."

"So what happened at the party that was so unusual?" I asked.

"That night there was only this hard-core group of us left."

"I was *so* bombed. Margy was bombed. Wouldn't you say, Margy? You were so bombed. Susie started giving all of us rides on the motorcycle, around the yard, down the driveway."

As they talked they consumed their tunafish sandwiches and Diet Cokes. Identical lunches, they had to share an apartment, and probably had adjoining desks. Now red-haired Margy was popping seedless red grapes into her mouth and brown-haired Carol was eating a banana.

"Somebody got hurt?" I asked.

"No, no, nothing wild or dangerous. Susie started teasing Senator Bridges, daring him to take a ride with her, until finally he did it, got on, and off they roared, with him on the back, hanging on around her waist. He was wearing just a pair of trunks and Susie had on this really mean bikini. Remember, Margy?"

"They must have made quite a sight," I said.

"They went out the driveway and didn't come back," Margy said between grapes. "Maybe twenty minutes passed and no sight of them. We began to worry, until we see Susie riding back alone but, get this, followed by a local cop car."

"Where was Bridges? In the car?"

Margy held out a hand filled with grapes. I took one. "Not in the car," she said. "Not in sight. We didn't know what had happened but we covered for him."

"We told the police he and his wife were out of town and let us use the place for a party," Carol said. "Margy, remember how I invited the policemen to have a Coke? I knew they couldn't drink on duty, but they were young, about our age."

"Here's what happened," Margy said. "Susie went up the road from the house about a mile or so and took a left on a dirt road she came upon. At the end of it, when she tried to turn the motorcycle around, she let the motor die on her. She was trying to get it started when the cops drove up. See, she didn't know it, but that road is a lovers' lane, has been for years and years, and the cops drive in there now and then to chase the kids out."

"So there was Dolph Bridges sitting on a motorcycle in lovers' lane with Susan Jacobs. Half naked," I said.

"He thought about his reputation. You can't blame

184

him," Margy said. "He jumped off the back of the motor-cycle and ran into the bushes the second he saw the flashing light on the top of the police car."

"And Susan Jacobs took the heat?"

"Like she'd been doing it all her life. The police let her go with a warning," Margy said.

"They thought it was funny, too," Carol added. "Also, she was quite a sight in that bikini."

"Ten minutes after the cops left, Senator Bridges came back, out of the woods."

"And, boy, did he get a ragging from the rest of us. Remember that, Margy? Remember how we really let him have it?"

"I'll bet you did," I said.

"The next Monday some of us chipped in at the office and bought a toy motorcycle and put two little stuffed bears on it and put it on his desk. He thought that was really funny, too."

"You said his wife wasn't there. Did you say that?"

"She wasn't at the party."

"If she'd been there, he never would have got on the back of that motorcycle," Carol said. "At least, that's what I think. What do you think, Margy?"

14

H<small>E WASN'T HARD TO</small> find, not with a name like that.
The base personnel office at Quantico in-
formed me that my nephew, Lance Corporal Randall
Randall, had recently been transferred to the marine
barracks in Washington, where he was a member of the
ceremonial platoon. After scanning his assignment
sheet, the duty officer at the marine barracks told me the
ceremonial platoon was at Arlington National Cemetery
that afternoon, participating in the funeral services for a
retired Marine Corps major general. It took me all of
fifteen minutes and a couple of bucks to find this out on
a pay phone in the Senate cafeteria. I took a cab.

The services were over, the family had departed and
the platoon of marines was about to board a military bus
to return to the barracks when I arrived at the cemetery.
It's a quiet place, well tended, but, like the eye of a storm,
home for men who died in violent battle.

I found the platoon sergeant and showed him my old

Marine Corps ID card. I keep it, tattered and faded though it is, because it can do a lot for you at times. Once a marine, always a marine. And what's wrong with that?

"Korea, I see by the dates. A little before my time," he said.

"Second Battalion, First Marine Division."

"What can I do for you?"

"You got a guy named Randall Randall in the ceremonial platoon. I'd like a word with him."

"Debts? Trouble? If that's the case, you go strictly through channels."

"Nothing like that at all. Nothing against him. I just need a little information he can provide."

He hesitated. All creases, uniform and face, the sergeant had the mean mother-hen look of a boot camp DI written all over him. "Randall is a real high-quality marine, you know what I mean? He's also sort of special."

"What do you mean by that?"

"He's right over there, tall kid with black hair. Find out for yourself. You got five minutes before I move this bus out."

Lance Corporal Randall was six two and lean as a greyhound, and his dress-blue uniform was beyond being perfectly pressed. It looked as if it had been drawn on his body by somebody using a draftsman's ruler. The black hair was regulation cut. I couldn't imagine a wig on his head. He was standing in the shade of an oak tree, smoking a nonfilter cigarette, and when I approached him and introduced myself he rubbed the cigarette against the trunk of the tree, putting it out, field-stripped it, came to attention and said, "Sir!" He was maybe twenty-five, young enough to be my son.

"It is my sad duty to inform you that an acquaintance of yours, Miss Susan Jacobs, has died in an accident," I told him.

"Yes, sir! Thank you, sir! Sorry to hear that, sir!" His response didn't especially surprise me. He had seen me talking with his sergeant, and young marines such as he are drilled to respond with alacrity to anyone cloaked in the thinnest raiment of authority. You never knew, the guy could be a senior commissioned officer out of uniform. It was what he said after that which surprised me. "May our Savior, the good Lord Jesus, have mercy on her soul, even though she was of the Jewish faith, *sir!*" he said.

"I know you two were close."

"Thank you, *sir!* I appreciate it, *sir!* Even though we were no longer close, *sir!*"

"A young enlisted marine has a hard time competing with a United States senator, I guess. Especially when he's the girl's boss, to boot."

"No comment, *sir!*"

"Susan died in a water accident up in Massachusetts last week."

"The Lord giveth and the Lord taketh away. Blessed be the name of the Lord, sir!"

"Reborn, are you?"

"Praise the Lord. On the tenth day of May at revival services in Arlington. The first day of the rest of my life, sir."

"Look too young and too good in that uniform to have done much sinning, Randall."

"Beer and motorcycles are the tools of the devil, *sir*!"

"I know Susan fell in with Senator Bridges after that party at his home last summer. You must have felt pretty bad about it."

"Fucked his brains out for him, sir! She was a harlot, sir."

"You never saw Susan again after that party?"

"Yes, sir. A few times, sir. Before I had been saved, sir."

"You mean last fall? After her summer romance with Senator Bridges was over? When his wife came back home?"

"Thou sayest."

"Did she break off the relationship? Did she get tired of him? Or afraid?"

"Just the opposite, sir. She was one more angry Jewish harlot, sir."

"I'll bet she was. So she got back in touch with you and you took her back."

"Thou sayest."

"Randall, I'm not Pontius Pilate and you're not Jesus Christ, okay?"

The other members of the ceremonial platoon were boarding the bus. "Time to haul ass, Randall," his sergeant called.

"I'm sorry, kid," I said.

"It don't mean nothing to me, sir. Not anymore. I'm with a fine Christian girl who led me into the arms of my Savior. Blessed be the name of the Lord."

"That's wonderful. I wish you good luck."

"She's pretty as a picture, not a drop of Jewish blood runs through her veins. She teaches Sunday school and not the first taste of beer has ever passed through her lips either."

"I'm sorry to have to be the one to tell you about Susan."

"That's okay, sir. But I ain't one bit sorry to hear it and I know that Donnie Lee won't be either because she says I bore her when I talk about how Susan and I carried on with beer and drugs and motorcycles when I was living a life of sin. Before my conversion, I would have told you you made my day, sir." He was standing at attention and trying hard not to cry, lips trembling, eyes beginning to redden.

"The medical examiner says she suffered no pain." A lie. I didn't know.

"When they examined her body, was she pregnant again, sir?"

"No. You said *again*. Was she pregnant last fall?"

He didn't answer me. He didn't have to.

"Is that your problem? Were you rolling around town last fall on your motorcycle with your pregnant sweetheart hanging on behind? Pregnant with Dolph Bridges's child?"

"Randall, get your ass on this bus!" the sergeant yelled.

"What's your connection with all this?" Randall asked.

"I'm a friend of Susan's older sister."

The sergeant walked over to us. "Okay, marine, you've used up your welcome."

"We're all through. Thanks."

Randall reached into his hip pocket, pulled out a thin wallet and from that extracted a small, worn brass key. "You might give this to her sister because I won't be having no use for it anymore."

Lance Corporal Randall Randall then did a right face and marched to the bus. He climbed on board without looking back at me.

I looked down at the key he had placed in my hand.

"I told you he's special," the sergeant said.

She'd lived in a small apartment house in the four hundred block of First Street, southeast, according to a phone book I found inside the Custis-Lee Mansion, and I had the cabdriver take me there directly from the cemetery. Her building was across the street from a restaurant named Bullfeathers, and I stopped there, sat at one of the outside sidewalk tables and had a club sandwich and a glass of iced tea, keeping an eye on the apartment house while I ate. Good thing, too.

Back in the early sixties, when the war in Vietnam was heating up, I spent three months there on assignment. One nice morning I went for a ride down into the delta with a young political officer from the American embassy I had got to know. You could still do that in those days, in certain areas, as long as you got back to Saigon before sundown. We stopped in a village to buy some fruit for lunch from a street vendor, and I was counting out the piasters to pay for it when my friend from the embassy said quietly, "Don't look up, but take a glance across the street."

There was a column of nine or ten little guys making its way through the village. They were all dressed in black pajamas and tennis shoes and they had bumps and bulges under their blouses. A Viet Cong patrol it was, out for an unusual daylight stroll. They paid us no mind and went on their way, but we got out of there in one hell of a hurry.

I felt much the same way that afternoon, sitting at my table at the restaurant. I paid my bill and was about to stand up and walk across the street to the apartment house when its front door opened and two black men walked out. One was a skinny guy, a snappy dresser in his black double-breasted suit, red satin shirt and gray lizard-skin boots. The other was a big bruiser who looked like he got his clothes out of the bin at Goodwill.

They glanced around, right out of the movies, before they got into a Chevrolet that had a Hertz sticker on its windshield and drove away.

I didn't work as a newspaper reporter in Chicago for twenty-five years for nothing. I know top-of-the-line mob muscle when I see it, and I had been looking at it. Unless you have urgent business, steer clear of such people. They would as soon kill you as look at you. Suddenly thirsty, I ordered another glass of iced tea.

I waited thirty minutes. They didn't return. They could have been Washington-based, of course, but the rental car convinced me they were out-of-town talent who probably were on their way now to the airport to catch the early afternoon flight back to Chicago, Detroit or New York.

Finally I made myself get up and cross the street. The name plate at the door said S. Jacobs lived in 2-D, a second-floor walk-up. The key Randall Randall had given me fit and turned in the lock easily, an old, long-used key the lock knew well.

Susan Jacobs's apartment obviously had not yet been visited by her older sister. Susan's things were still there. The place had been tossed by experts.

I turned immediately and left the apartment, letting the door close behind me and not bothering to search the place. I knew I wouldn't find anything after those two godzillas had had their turn.

I took a cab to the airport and caught the four o'clock

Eastern shuttle to New York. At six-thirty that evening I was in the Café des Artistes, having a drink with Lala Powers.

"I happened to be in town on business and I thought I'd give you a buzz," I told her.

"Come off it. Don't try to put me on, friend. You're working on that *Times* article."

"You're right. I'm doing a little research."

"That's more like it. Be honest with me. Believe it or not, I'm a very truthful person. Sometimes it gets me in trouble. I know I shoot my mouth off too much."

"Everything all patched up with Billy?"

"That asshole. For the first time in my life I've told a man I'm through with him unless he quits drinking. He says he's thinking about it."

"Where are you off to tonight? You look like a million dollars. That dress glitters."

"I'm covering a rock concert and a big-name party afterwards. Mostly the Euro-trash set, but people seem to love to see them on the tube and my producer digs the scene." She put her middle finger in her mouth, looked me in the eye, and sucked it slowly. "Know what I mean?"

"No. You're much too subtle for me."

"He likes to get invited, make the scene, and he hopes he will if he puts them on the tube often enough. The asshole wants to be a regular, if you can imagine. A couple of French movie stars will be there. I can make a spot out of it for *Beautiful People*."

"How's your spot on Helen Bridges coming along?"

"It's ancient history as far as I'm concerned, written and tracked, and in the hands of a producer and tape editor."

"A shattering exposé, I'm sure."

"I called her everything except a carbon copy of the Virgin Mary. If she gets into the White House, *I* want in the White House, by God. I want in bed with her, in the Lincoln bedroom, with both of us in flannel nightgowns and our hair up in curlers. With her telling me how King Whositz tried to finger her under the table during a state dinner. And what she really thinks of that dyke her husband appointed to his cabinet."

"Money in the bank."

"You have no idea how much, Up-Country."

The bar was filled with its usual after-work crowd. The Café des Artistes is a hangout for ABC news people, the way Hurley's once was for the NBC folks. Network types are an emotional, insecure, talkative tribe, and the air was filled with chatter about rumored budget cuts and layoffs, stupid story assignments and idiotic assignment editors who said no to brilliant concepts. There were also frequent references to insensitive cuts and changes ordered by show executive producers and to the stupidity of nationally known on-air talent.

Beautiful People was an independent, syndicated production, but the show's executive offices and editing rooms were in the same neighborhood and its staff members naturally gravitated to the same bar.

"You seem to know everything, Lala," I said. "I want to ask you something in total confidence. Has there been any talk in the past few months about Helen and Dolph?"

Lala fluttered her eyelashes. "Goodness! What have *you* heard? Look, they're together now, aren't they? What are you trying to do, stir up trouble?"

"I'm not talking about divorce or even separation. I'm talking about strain on the marriage."

"Why do you want to know?"

"I'm not out for blood. I don't write for the *National Enquirer*. I'm trying to bring the guy into focus in my own mind."

"I quite understand. I know the high-and-mighty *New York Times* doesn't deal in common gossip. It's concerned about higher things. So, why did you come all the way to New York to see me?"

"Curiosity, pure and simple."

She threw her hands up. "Why didn't you say so in the first place? Sure, I heard there was a little trouble. What else is new? Hell, everybody married I know has trouble. I think the talk started, and there wasn't all that much of it, when Helen went to a tennis camp late last summer and early fall, in Arizona somewhere, the paid guest of Buffy Whitfield, as I understand it. She plays tennis all the time in Washington with her."

"Any talk about a girlfriend on the side? Dolph doesn't have the reputation of a guy who screws around."

"Mac, take it from somebody who's been around the

track a few times. A woman never knows whose hand is going to land on her leg under a Washington dinner-party table. Or who's going to ask you out to lunch. Or try to slide his leg between yours when you're dancing at tonight's charity ball."

"Sodom on the Potomac."

"The young studs, just elected, with lots of publicity when they arrive in town, a *Style* profile in the *Post*, say, about this Nevada asshole and his wife, Rusty, and how they gave up their big-sky life-style to come to Washington with three kids the size of bull elks to serve the public good, no matter how much they hate the East. That guy screwed all the secretaries in his law office, most of the volunteers on his campaign staff, and he thinks he's doing you a favor to give it to you in Washington. You almost have to make an appointment."

I waved at the waiter and raised two fingers. He nodded.

"And the older ones who've been around almost take it for granted," Lala said. "They try to feel you up in the library. You offer your cheek for a hello kiss and they stick their tongues in your mouth. They're all over you."

"It sounds like a jungle down there."

"Most politicians I've known are horny, and I've known a lot of them. It goes with the territory. A lot of wives and kids go away from Washington in the summer because of the climate, go back home, to the beach, to the mountains. They leave behind summer bachelors, so called, who eat frozen beef hash and then hit the singles bars, or raid their offices. And there are thousands of single women to choose from."

"You're saying if Dolph had a fling it wouldn't be all that unusual. I close my eyes and I see hordes of lecherous pols on the prowl in Georgetown bars."

The waiter brought our second round of drinks, maneuvering his way to our table from the bar. Vodka martinis on the rocks, Lala's choice and it had sounded fine to me.

"Who's the chick?" she asked.

"Who said there was one?"

"Otherwise you wouldn't be here. You think I'm stupid?" She laughed. "You come to me checking on gossip. You're out of your league, Down Home."

"Teach me, guide me."

"Up yours. I'm talking about gossip. Lunch. Phone calls from New York to Los Angeles, from Washington to the Hamptons. It's a party line. A big national gossip party line."

"So what's the latest on Dolph Bridges?"

"Nothing lately. There was a feeling sometime back that something was going on, but nobody could ever come up with a name. Unless there's a woman of some standing involved, it's, it's . . ." Lala waved a hand in exasperation.

"Just a guy screwing his secretary?"

"Exactly."

"Helen?"

"Ball the tennis pro on the side? It never got back to me. She's more wrapped up in her exercise and her diet than anything else. That and her image. Washington is filled with political couples like them, although not many of them get within striking distance of the White House. That ups the ante."

"I've known my share of politicians and their wives. They play a role the voters buy and it gets them elected, which forces them to play the same roles forever to keep winning."

"Lots of them enjoy it, or come to enjoy it. To me it would be like holding a Tupperware party seven after-noons a week, fifty-two weeks a year."

"Helen's not a Tupperware saleswoman."

"Helen never had to play in the political minor leagues. She married a United States senator secure in office, popular at home. That is to die for. Dolph's so popular in Illinois he could have campaigned for reelection to the Senate wearing a gold lamé gown and won going away. So Helen never had to make it to the lunch-eon groups or the coffees or the wine-and-cheese par-ties."

"Maybe that seasons and weathers a First Lady."

"Bullshit. Jackie Kennedy never did it. Don't think of Dolph and Helen as a team of matched horses. They may be pulling the same load, heading for the same barn, they may be together but they're not matched. How do you like that barnyard illustration, Hayseed?"

15

I T CAME OUT OF the fog making about sixty miles an hour and it sailed over the chain-link backup fence. "That's a little better, Bubba," I said. "Keep working on that control. Let's try it again."

I dug into my back pocket, pulled out another ball and tossed it to him. "This time try to keep it lower. Think about where you're going to throw it."

He reared back in his windup. The morning fog swirled around him, temporarily obscuring his body again. The baseball came out of the fog, but this time it hit the ground halfway between the pitcher's mound and home plate, where I was squatting.

He was twelve years old, almost six feet tall, and he weighed around two hundred pounds, a baby Valenzuela who had a fastball that would trail smoke when he was a couple of years older. But he was wild.

Bubba Olsen was the son of Jimmy Olsen, the clerk of the Barnstable County probate court, and Noah Simmons's nephew. I could see Noah the kid in him, which probably was why I didn't mind spending time working with him on his control at the North Walpole Little League park. Back in the olden days I pitched one season of Class A ball, Clinton, Iowa, which put me right up there alongside Grover Cleveland Alexander as far as Jimmy Olsen was concerned. Jimmy, a little guy just over five feet, was a baseball nut and coach of the Little League team. Bubba was supposed to be his secret weapon that season, but Jimmy had about given up on him.

"Get the ball and bring it to me," I told the boy.

He did as he was told. Bubba was not a sullen, uncooperative boy. He was eager and anxious to please, a good kid.

"You holding it the way I told you when you throw it?" He nodded. "Well, like I told you, forget about curves and sinkers. You're too young, you'll ruin your arm. Just throw a fastball, that's all. And don't worry. Don't worry about the guy who's just got a hit off you or the guy who's coming up. Don't worry about if you're going to hit the batter or if he's going to hit the ball, or the way he's wig-wagging the bat, or what people are yelling. Concentrate. Here's what you're thinking about, this catcher's mitt. That's all. Now, try it again."

Bubba trudged back to the mound, no quitter, and tried it again, and again, a little better, but not much, each time.

It was a foggy morning, fog left over after a foggy night. People who love Cape Cod and enjoy extolling its beauty and pleasures somehow neglect to mention the fog. The Massachusetts peninsula is a good way out in the North Atlantic Ocean and about a hundred miles off its elbow the Gulf Stream runs, so there is fog, sometimes in patches, sometimes in blankets. It comes and goes. It had come the night before.

It was raining in New York when I left Lala and caught a cab to La Guardia, where the Eastern shuttle to Boston sat on the ground for an hour before we took off. At Logan we circled for another hour before landing because of the air traffic backup, and all flights to Hyannis had been canceled. I ended up spending the night at the Logan Hilton, sleeping in my underwear, and flew across the bay the next morning. Kate was still in Chicago with Martha Jacobs, and when I walked in the house the phone was ringing, Jimmy threatening to banish Bubba unless his control improved and imploring me to work with him that morning. So there I was.

We had company, wild Bubba and I. Dolph Bridges sat in the red Jeep in the parking lot and watched us while we worked. I said nothing, gave no sign that I had spotted him. He made no move to join us, not until I told the boy, "That's enough for today," and sent him away on his bike to the public library to look for an illustrated book on pitching, told him to look for a gray-haired lady volunteer and feel free to use my name. As soon as

Bubba left, Dolph got out of the Jeep and approached me.

"How'd you find me?" I asked.

"That boy's father is telling everybody in town that a former big-league pitcher named McFarland is coaching his son."

"I had a hunch you'd be looking for me. The miracle of long-distance direct dialing. Take Davis Putney. He picks up his phone in his office down in Washington, dials, and he's talking to you, just like that."

Dolph smiled. "Lala, too." He was wearing jeans, sneakers, a blue polo shirt and a yellow rain parka.

"I remember, you used to screw her."

"I've come to talk with you seriously, Mac."

"Oh. In that case, why don't you start by telling the truth. I don't believe you anymore, Dolph."

"I don't blame you. That's why I'm here, to talk man-to-man. We're more or less the same age. I think we understand each other."

"Don't try to stroke me. This isn't the floor of the Senate. And more than a vote is at stake here."

He looked at me steadily. "You've been poking around."

"And you've been lying to me."

"I'm here to straighten that out, to tell you everything, and to ask something from you. I screwed that girl last summer."

"I already know that. Dolph, I know a lot."

"I never messed around in Washington. Last summer was the one and only time, and I fell into it. Helen and I were having a little trouble. We worked it out. We're okay now."

"You knocked Susan Jacobs up."

"I took care of it. Christ, this isn't the fifties. Abortion isn't that unusual."

"Maybe you paid for it. But a kid young enough to be your own son held her hand and walked her through it."

"Mac, she came on to me."

"I'm not faulting you for laying her. I know you're not exactly the first presidential candidate who got a little on the side."

"I could name names."

"How long did it go on?"

"Last summer, weekends, that's all. I called a halt to it when Helen came home from that tennis camp. After that I never saw Susan again, except in the office hallways from time to time. She'd smile and wave. It was just a lark for both of us."

"You never told Helen about her?"

"Christ, no!"

"And you never had contact with her again until she appeared on the patio at the Munro house here that night, the night she died? You didn't know she was living at the restaurant right across the Cut? You don't know why she showed up at the dinner party that night, kissed you, told you not to worry, that her lips were sealed?"

"No. I swear it."

"I can see why you're so worried about it. I don't believe you and neither would anybody else. Smart guy, used to be senator, wants to be president, asks us to buy that story?"

"Which is exactly why I'm trying to keep it covered up. What choice do I have? I ask you."

A light rain had begun to fall. "The North Walpole police chief thinks Susan Jacobs was murdered. I told you that on the plane. He could ask the district court to order an inquest."

"Which would fry my ass."

"And I'm the loose cannon on the deck. This is the second time you've told me that."

"This time you have all the facts."

"Which also is what you said the last time." I threw up my hands. "Fornicate all politicians!" When he offered me his hand I refused to shake it. "*Is* this all of it, Dolph?" I asked him.

We walked together toward our cars in the parking lot. The rain was coming down harder. "No, it's not, not all. I want you to consider something. Think about becoming my press secretary."

I stopped walking, looked at him. "You have got to be kidding."

"Not now. After all this blows over. After you've written your article for the *Times*. Next fall, months from now. I've thought about this a great deal, Mac. Billy's not up to it, not when the big boys move in. You are. And you don't have a job, nothing regular. We're close to the same age, from the same part of the country. You know the territory, presidential campaigns. The people in your business know you as a person of integrity. I've thought about it. I need you, Mac."

I didn't answer him.

"The pay's at a rate of seventy-five a year. Of course, if I win, I'd ask you to go in the White House with me as press secretary."

"I'll pretend you never made the offer. Don't make it again."

Dolph walked through the rain over to the red Jeep, opened the driver's door. "All I'm asking is that you don't say yes or no yet. Think about it. We'll talk again a couple of months from now and not until then. Okay?"

He waved and pulled away. I stood there getting wet. I was pretty sure the son of a bitch had tried to bribe me.

MouMou was under the bed, hiding from me. She knew that Kate was out of the house.

I ignored the old bitch, never called her name out loud. I took off my wet clothes and left them in the bathroom hamper, put on a pair of old khakis that had seen better days and a white shirt that had holes in the elbows, went down to the kitchen, opened a bottle of beer and made myself my favorite noonday sandwich, liverwurst and a thick slice of onion on pumpernickel bread with Dijon mustard. Heaven. My session with Bubba Olsen had left me hungry.

I sat at the kitchen table, ate my lunch, and tried to think. Nothing. There weren't that many people involved, after all, not exactly a cast of thousands. I thought of them as characters in a play, the set that steak cookout on the patio with the South Seas torches burning. Nothing, except Susan Jacobs tracing around.

I took them one at a time.

Eliot More. My hunch was that Dolph had nothing for her. He wouldn't make her White House chief of staff, perhaps offer her nothing of substance. Still, a presidential win, with all the attendant publicity, would guarantee her fame and great fortune as a political consultant for years to come, big suite of offices on K Street, big name about town. But Eliot struck me as a measured, controlled person and I couldn't see her driving that VW around with Susan out cold in the seat beside her. Eliot could have done it, but I didn't think so.

Billy Nolan without Dolph would be on the bricks because of the booze, in my opinion. With Dolph, being on the staff, he could still think of himself as the old Billy, and after the election Dolph would find something for him that would allow him to hold his head up, something at USIA maybe. But Billy had confessed to Father Terry Riley. Billy told me about the steak cookout. Billy was my friend.

Thomas Duncan was hungry for new respectability

and, in the White House, Dolph could give him that with the stroke of a pen, his signature on a letter of appointment. Was that motivation enough? I didn't know.

Charls Munro, Dolph's money man, and his wife, Dody. Forget it. They didn't even know who Susan Jacobs was.

Helen Bridges wanted to be First Lady of Washington, Lala said. She was a poor woman of good family, a good athlete who swam daily in the sound. Power and privilege was almost within her grasp. Did she want it that badly?

There was Dolph, the liar, who wanted me to be his press secretary.

The physical whereabouts that night of all of them was unknown to me.

MouMou needed attention. She hadn't been let out of the house for thirty-six hours, but she took orders from nobody but Kate, and Kate wasn't home. It was time.

I got my things from the storage room adjoining the kitchen, a push broom, a flashlight and a pair of leather work gloves, walked up to the bedroom, got down on my knees beside the bed and shined the light in the old dog's red eyes.

"You hate me, don't you," I said. "You'd like to try to bite me with the one tooth you've got left in your head. Forget it." I spoke in a pleasant, mild tone of voice because Kate insisted that was needed to establish a loving relationship between the two of us.

The dog growled at me.

"Kate's not home," I told her. "It's just you and me,

you bitch, so come out from under that bed. If you don't, MouMou gives Daddy here no recourse except—*the broom!*"

Another growl. She knew what was coming.

I pushed the broom under the bed. "Get out from under there, damn you!"

The telephone on the bedside table started ringing. I reached up from the floor and took it off the receiver. It was Noah. "What are you doing? Fighting a burglar?"

"I'm trying to get MouMou outside for a piss call."

"When you manage it, why don't you meet me at the Binnacle for a drink."

"Sure. What's up?"

"I've figured out what Susan Jacobs meant when she said she was tracing around," he said.

16

NOAH WAS WAITING FOR me when I got there, sitting at a table just inside the open front door, sipping a Coke and looking through the plate-glass window at the crowd of young people in the park across the street. The kids were standing in a circle on the lawn, listlessly kicking around a small cloth bag filled with beach sand.

The Binnacle had assumed its summertime beachtown look. No longer the winter hangout for locals, it was filled with strangers. Like all the other merchants on Main Street, Nickey was going for the tourist dollar. Extra waitresses had been hired. Mary Beth, the regular waitress, had become a receptionist. They were all wearing Nickey's new summer getups, including bow ties and straw boaters perched on their heads.

I sat down in a chair across from Noah. "The park's filled with kids. I guess school's finally out," I said.

"I used to hang out there in the park when I was their age," he said. "I don't know. Summers can be lonely somehow here for the local kids."

"Are they a problem?"

"Teenagers with time on their hands are always a problem."

"Drugs?"

"Some do. Some don't. Pot mostly. A little coke when they can afford it. The summer kids are more of a problem usually, because they have more money."

"On the phone you sounded like you'd solved a mystery."

He offered me a copy of that day's Cape Cod *Times*. "Look at the story on the top of the first page of the second section."

I found it and read it. "I have the feeling he's the sort of person who's got to keep busy wherever he is." The story said that Charls Munro, Dolph Bridges's financial chairman, had acquired a majority interest in a large shopping center in Hyannis.

"Read it again. Carefully. You see he's identified as Charls Munro the Second. Roman numeral two."

"That means he's not a junior, not named after his father. He's probably named after his grandfather. He's got a gold identification bracelet with Chas Dos engraved on it. So what?"

"There's a third. A son. Charls Munro the Third. His nickname is Tres. He's Munro's only child."

I looked at the name again in the newspaper and thought about it. "The second and the third. Dos and tres. Tres, Spanish for three. That's what Susan Jacobs was saying on the patio that night, wasn't it? Billy Nolan was full of beer and misunderstood her. Is Tres around? That's what she was saying. Not *tracing* around."

"He's known around here only by his nickname. He lives on the Cape year-round. The funny spelling of the first name was what put me off."

"It sounds like Susan Jacobs knew him, she saw the lights and the people on the patio and maybe thought he was giving a party without her."

"The timing's right. She got in town a few days before the Senator and his people arrived. The house was empty."

"Charls Dos and Charls Tres."

"What really connected it for me was the drugs found in her body."

"You think this Tres Munro gave them to her?"

"Mac, he's a fucking pusher."

A young man, bone-skinny and in his early twenties, pulled up at the entrance of the park across the street on a black Yamaha motorcycle. He had long black matted hair and he was wearing all black, black boots, black corduroy jeans and a black muscle shirt. Both his arms were tattooed from his wrists to his shoulders, tattooed not with anchors and eagles but with what looked like snakes and dragons.

"There he is," Noah said. "I wanted you to get a look at him. He usually shows up around the park about now."

"He sell to the kids?"

"He sells to anybody who'll buy from him. My guess is he gets the junk in Providence. I've been trying to nail him for months. But as far as I can tell, he deals off and on. Nothing very big and nothing regular."

"He looks like a user, too. Skinny. You think he was with Susan Jacobs that night?"

"Let's see what we can find out. Come on."

We left the Binnacle and walked across the street to Tres Munro, who was watching the young people play in the park. He paid no attention to us.

Noah gave the motorcycle a long, close inspection. "Maybe I ought to get some of these for the force," he said to me. "They'd be great in summer traffic jams."

Tres Munro was smoking a cigarette. "Those kids can really keep that sand bag in the air a long time," he said. "It looks like fun."

"Charls, I'm going to walk down the street with my friend here to the police station," Noah said, squatting to inspect the tires of the motorcycle. "You wait five minutes and follow me. I want to have a talk with you. Don't even think about not showing up."

Noah obviously didn't intend to arrest him for dealing, not now, and he wanted him to know it. That five minutes would give him plenty of time to dump anything he might be carrying. The big police chief turned and walked away without another word. I followed him and we strolled down Main Street, with him saying hello every few feet along the way.

The entire village of North Walpole was coming alive like a flowering bush following a long and bitter winter's sleep. You could feel it, see it happening.

Many of the cars that crowded Main Street had out-of-state license tags and the parking places were all filled. Nearly all the summer shops and eating places, closed and boarded for the winter, were open for business, with menus posted on the windows, with pots of flowers and freshly painted signs, and with outdoor displays of things offered for sale, quilts, leather sandals, scenic watercolors. The sidewalks were filled with strangers, strangers who seemed to know Noah, *summer people*.

Noah had posted policemen, specials he called them, at two of the busiest crossings to handle the increased crowds. "How's it going?" he asked the one who was at the Alden variety store.

"So far no problem. But you can tell the difference with every passing day."

We were drinking coffee in Styrofoam cups when Tres Munro was shown into Noah's office. He had a first-class look of innocence on his face, either genuine or that fake quizzical look people try to fool you with. I couldn't decide which.

"I assume five minutes gave you time to stash your goods. No search," Noah told him.

"I have no idea—"

"I'm not busting you. Sit down."

It was an order and Tres Munro knew it. He sat. He folded his hands in his lap like a choirboy.

"I read in the paper where your dad's bought a big shopping center over in Hyannis," Noah said.

"I wouldn't know, sir."

"He doesn't discuss business with you, Charls? You ought to insist. A small businessman like yourself could pick up some pointers."

"I'm banned from the house."

"Is that a fact? Because you're a dealer. And an addict?"

"You've got the look. You look like a concentration camp survivor," I said. I guess he thought I was a cop, too. He looked at me but didn't challenge me.

"I've quit," he said.

"How old were you when you started?" I asked him.

"Twelve. In Chicago."

"How old are you now?" Noah asked him.

Tres thought about it. "Twenty-three. Or twenty-four. Time passes."

He looked addled, almost brain-damaged. I did a newspaper series once on young people like him when I worked in Chicago. Every big city has hundreds. They get hooked before they can get a hard-on. Their parents can't control them, but they don't reject them, either, because they're so young. Youth for them is a walk on a foggy night, and I guessed that was why Tres was watching the kids in the park with such interest while they kicked the sand bag around. By the time their parents have tried everything without success and finally kicked them out, they are in their late teens or early twenties, but emotionally and intellectually they are still the kids they never were, arrested adolescents with an attention span of maybe fifteen seconds on a good day.

"Twenty-three or twenty-four. That's a little young for Susan Jacobs," Noah said, getting right down to the business at hand.

"You remember what her sister said," I said. "Age didn't matter to her. Young, old."

"What'd she do, Tres? Trade you pussy for pills?" Noah had taken some sort of mean pill himself. He didn't talk like that.

"I don't understand," Tres said.

"Susan Jacobs. The young woman who drowned in that VW off Cranberry House. You knew her."

"No, I didn't."

"You dealt to her."

"I don't deal."

"And Pluto doesn't bark at the door when the postman comes."

"From Washington, a newcomer. Very pretty," I said.

"Oh. Sure."

"Listen to me," Noah said. "I know you've made up a story and gone over it. Forget it. Just tell me the truth, about what happened that night with the two of you."

"I don't remember," Tres said.

"Noah, he may not," I said. "Tres uses heroin."

"I quit that shit, mister!"

"You mean you want to quit and know you should."

216

"I *have* quit!"

"Then why haven't your parents welcomed you back home with open arms?"

The boy—I couldn't bring myself to think of him as a man—stood and stalked about Noah's office. "I got things to do," he muttered.

"I don't know how much you have to deal with this here on the Cape," I said to Noah.

"Not much here in North Walpole, thank God."

"He's what they call in Chicago jonesy, getting the craving for a fix. He's nervous and jumpy, up the wall. His mind goes back and forth. He finds it hard to remember what you say from one minute to the next."

Noah nodded in understanding. "Tres, I know you spent the fall and winter around here. I saw you on the street now and then and I heard about you. When did your folks kick you out?"

"The end of last summer. Not my mother. My dad. He threw me out."

I thought about Charls Munro II. I could see him doing just that.

"You couldn't go home to Chicago with them. You didn't stay at the house here. I checked it out from outside now and again over the winter."

"I got a job as a busboy at the Hyatt in Hyannis. I rented a pad there."

"The chief can check all that out," I told him.

217

"He can check. The job fell through after New Year's. No business."

"So to support yourself and to feed your habit, you started dealing," Noah said.

"Just a little. I stayed at the house out at the Cut this spring when my money gave out. I broke in. I got in touch with my mom. She let me. You can check with her. I wasn't breaking any law. It's our house. And she didn't tell my dad, either. He still doesn't know, so don't check with him."

"And in May, with the nice weather we had, what happened? Did you and Susan Jacobs become kind of waving friends?" Noah asked. "She was lying on the patio at the restaurant, sunbathing, and you were right across the Cut, hanging out around the pool. Is that what happened?"

"I didn't try to make out with her or anything. She waved first."

"You yell across to her? 'Come on over.' Or did she?"

Tres was pacing about the room once again.

"Did you ride your motorcycle over there where she was?" I asked.

"She liked bikes. We rode on it around the whole Cape."

"She liked cocaine, too, didn't she? And ludes," Noah said.

"She wasn't a coke head or anything like that. Not like some girls from your precious North Walpole I could name."

"But she liked it. And you liked her. You two used together. And drank together. Vodka. You saw a lot of each other for a few weeks."

"It was nothing heavy. Good friends."

"She thought you were having a party without her that night when she saw all the lights on the patio. Right?"

"That's what she said."

"Where'd you run into her?"

"Somewhere in town. She was cruising."

"Tres, you know she's dead, don't you?" I asked.

"I heard that," he said, as if he had heard she had moved to Falmouth.

"You ran into her by accident and she wanted a fix," Noah said.

"That's right. I had a couple of ludes on me, so I gave them to her."

"She drove away and you never saw her again. Is that what you're telling me?" Noah shouted. "I'm going to book you for murder. Do you want to be booked for murder?"

"My dad would kill me."

"Then tell me what happened that night!"

"Tres, how did you learn that senator from Washington was coming to your house on the Cut?" I asked.

Noah looked at me. He didn't say anything, but he was obviously annoyed because I had interrupted when he had Tres going.

"My mom," Tres said. "There wasn't a phone in the house, which fact you can easily verify by checking with the phone company. She sent me a telegram a few days before he came here."

"Suddenly you had no place to go."

Noah got it immediately. "Except the waitress bunkroom at the restaurant," he said. "So you moved in with Susan, didn't you?"

"I want to talk with my mom, please."

"We'll be doing that. First tell me what happened."

"I stayed there with her a night or two. She offered. I was sleeping on a mattress with a blanket, that's all. I wasn't there that *night*. I had business."

"Yeah, you were on Main Street pushing drugs," Noah said. "Or buying in Providence."

"Noah, I think I know why you couldn't find her anywhere in town after she left the party that night," I said. "She went back to the restaurant. Where Tres here showed up. They sat around there, drinking and swallowing Quaaludes, and decided to go for a ride in her car. With the bottle that was found in it. Isn't that right, Tres?"

"It was a nice night, moonlight and all. We weren't doing anything against the law."

"You drove the car?" Noah asked.

"She asked me to, so I did. I didn't break the speed limit. We rode around for about an hour."

"Then what happened?"

"Nothing. I mean, we went back to the restaurant. I went to bed and that's all I know."

"You said you want to call your mom?"

"I have the right to make one phone call. That's the law, isn't it?"

"Yes. But I don't think your mom. I'm going to call your dad."

Tres's eyes widened with terror. "Jesus, don't do that."

"I think I'd better."

"You don't know him. He'd go crazy. Please, don't."

"Then tell me the truth. The rest of what happened that night."

"I can't remember!"

"You lost control because of the booze and the ludes."

"I don't know. What time have you got? I got a job washing dishes at Cranberry House. I'm supposed to be there at five and Mr. Loory explodes if anybody's late. I've got to go pretty soon."

"You lost control and ran the car over the patio, through the railing, and into the water. Isn't that right?"

"I had a blackout."

"Don't hand me that crap. I don't believe it. Susan Jacobs was passed out in the seat beside you. When the car went in the water, the shock brought you out of it. You opened your door and got out. The water wasn't very deep and you were only out a little way."

"You got me. I don't even remember driving the car back to the restaurant."

Noah turned his back to him, facing me. "I don't know whether to believe him or not," he said softly.

"Tres, I've got a question," I said. "Where did you wake up the next morning?"

"Inside Saint John's Church, on a pew."

"Did you find your motorcycle outside the church?"

"Yes."

"So you drove it there from the restaurant."

"I told you, I don't remember."

"Did you get out of the car before it went into the water? And leave Susan in it?" Noah asked him.

"I'm at a total loss."

"Did you try to get her out of the car after it went into the water?"

"I don't know. I swear to you."

"That blackout happened at a very convenient time for you." Noah turned to me. "Manslaughter. Accidental homicide at least."

"Tres, close your eyes," I said. He obeyed me. "Say the first thing about that night at the restaurant that comes into your mind."

"Headlights?"

"I think I better call your mom," Noah said. "What's the number?"

Tres gave him our number at home. What a surprise.

17

"JUST TELL ME HOW a drug pusher mistakes you for his mother!" I shouted at Kate.

MouMou, who was lying in her lap, tried to go for me but Kate held her. "I don't know. Sometimes he confuses me with her. When he gets too much on his mind. Don't listen to Noah. He's a fanatic on the subject."

"It's something to be fanatical about."

It was later that afternoon and the evening sun was almost down. Kate was home, back from Chicago and Susan Jacobs's funeral, and looking more than a little tired after the drive in her car from the Boston airport. She was still wearing the clothes she had traveled in, a wrinkled tan linen suit. I told her about Tres Munro first thing.

We were sitting on the patio with a fat glass-globed candle for light, drinking gin and tonic.

"Tres is not a bad kid underneath, Mac," she said. "It's true I tried to help him."

"All mankind's mother." I sighed. "When did it start?"

"Last fall, before you showed up around here. His father kicked him out of the house on the Cut, so Tres stayed here on the Cape when the Munros moved back to Chicago at the end of the summer season."

"You should have told me about him."

"It was no big deal, nothing much to tell. When it got cold last fall, Father Riley found him sleeping in a pew at Saint John's. He asked me to help him. I know the manager of the Hyatt over in Hyannis and I got him on there, a phone call."

"And when he lost that job, he started pushing to pay for his habit."

"God, he uses. He admits it. But he's trying to quit on his own. And it isn't easy."

"He uses. And he deals."

"Off and on, I know. Pot and coke. But not as bad as Noah insists. The boy's trying. Nat Loory took him on as a dishwasher at Cranberry House as a favor to me, and Nat says he works hard and shows up on time."

"Not tonight. Noah's got him locked up. Your baby Tres has a convenient loss of memory about the night Susan Jacobs died. He's saying he suffered a blackout."

"Maybe he did."

"Do you think you could make him remember?"

"I could try. It might work better here. Not in that jail."

I called Noah at his office and he somewhat reluctantly agreed to bring the boy over to the house.

While we waited for the two of them to arrive, Kate told me she had never met or even talked to either of Tres's parents. But she knew a lot about him from what he had told her. From pot at twelve, bought around school, he quickly went on to anything he could find, to cocaine when he started hanging with an older user crowd when he was sixteen, finally to heroin.

Somehow the Munros managed to get him through high school in Chicago, but he refused to go on to college, exasperating his mother and angering his father. They couldn't do anything with him.

For the next five or six years he hung around, in and out of the big suburban Munro home in Chicago, sometimes on the Cape in the summers, floating from one half-ass job to another, briefly attending a community college, mooching and stealing from his mother, while his father, heavily involved in rapidly expanding business affairs, with more and more travel and with bigger and bigger bucks at stake, turned his face away from it all.

The blowup came when a new diamond dinner ring Munro bought as a wedding anniversary gift for his wife disappeared a few days after it was delivered to the North Walpole house by the Fifth Avenue store where he had ordered it. Tres swore his innocence, of course, but they didn't buy his story. His mother begged him to go to a treatment center but he refused. His father ordered him out of the house. Tres left home.

Kate was holding up her glass for a refill when the headlights of Noah's squad car swept over us briefly on the patio. He pulled the Ford Fairlane deeply into the driveway and parked beside our two cars in back. Noah and the boy got out and walked over to us.

Tres, I immediately noticed, had his long hair cut off—chopped was a better description—and he was wearing a new white long-sleeved dress shirt. Tres looked like Paul Muni in a Warner Bros. gangster movie.

"Well, here we are," Noah said gruffly.

"Who gave him the haircut? That cross-eyed guy that does lawns and ditches?" I asked.

"I keep a pair of clippers. I couldn't stand him in my jail looking like he did. He made it look like a dungeon. I bought the shirt at Pilgrim's."

"He certainly looks *different*," I said.

Tres stood before Kate, looking at her very tentatively, the kid caught with his hand in the cookie jar. I realized he was about as tall as I was, and the full-bodied white shirt he wore made him look heavier than he was.

"Go on, like I said on the way here. Talk to her," Noah said. He didn't like the idea of being there, wasn't comfortable with a woman, non-law, even Kate, doing his interrogative work for him.

"Mac, why don't you take Noah for a walk along the pond? See if you can spot any fish in the dark," Kate said. "Tres and I'll talk."

"Can't hurt," Noah said. He and I walked down the lawn to the edge of Clam Pond. Cutters had come that day and the grass smelled good.

"He won't call home. He's afraid of his old man," Noah said. "He claims he can't remember any more, either."

"Maybe Kate can get something out of him."

"Responsum faciamus. Non est quod apparatum."

"You know I can't understand that crap."

"There's more to it, I have a feeling."

"I remember you said you thought somebody searched through the girl's things at the restaurant."

"No prints. A good print is hard to find."

"Noah, there's something you should know. I went to Washington yesterday. Susan Jacobs's apartment has been searched, tossed."

"Tres Munro couldn't have done that, could he?"

"No, he couldn't. Two black guys, mob types. I saw them coming out of the place." I should have told him about Dolph Bridges's involvement with Susan Jacobs, but I didn't.

A fish, something, jumped in the salt pond, sending ripples. There was a half-moon, but it was partly cloudy.

"I'm going out and talk to Bridges tomorrow," he said.

"What are you going to charge the Munro boy with?"

"I'm thinking about it. I want to wait and see what Kate gets out of him. That business about seeing headlights has me worried."

That was when we heard the shots, two of them, up at

the house. "What the hell was that?" I shouted, but Noah was already running. I followed, as fast as I could.

We found them lying on the patio, about ten yards apart. Blood, lots of it, was all over. Tres Munro looked dead, contorted and silent, his mouth and eyes open. The front of the white shirt he was wearing was tattered and blood-red.

We ignored him, the way his needs had been ignored most of his short life, I guess, and ran to Kate. She was lying on her back beside the overturned cocktail table, moaning softly and bloody in big spots on her stomach and her left hip.

"Stay with her, Mac. Don't move her. I'll call the rescue squad," Noah said urgently. He ran into the house to use the phone.

I could barely breathe. My chest was tight. My teeth started chattering. I was kneeling beside Kate. MouMou, unharmed, stood over her, whining. Kate appeared to be unconscious.

Noah ran out. "They're on their way. Be here in a minute."

"They better be."

"You know them. They're trained paramedics, very good. They'll patch her up in the rescue vehicle on the way to the Hyannis hospital."

"They better, Noah."

"Try to take it easy."

I was crying. My eyesight was blurred by the tears.

"I'll get the bastard," Noah said. "This is out of hand."

"Remember Washington. There may be two of them. You better get them before I get my hands on them."

Noah walked over and examined Tres Munro's body. He didn't take long. "Poor kid," he said. "Twelve-gauge, I'd say. And at pretty close range. Out in the dark, on the other side of the driveway."

"The bastards were professionals," I managed to say.

"They must have parked in the front of the driveway, near the road, and slipped back here through the trees. But why hit a kid like that? It makes no sense."

We could hear the rescue squad siren from a distance away, coming down Clam Pond Drive full speed. Noah took another look at Kate, gave me a pat on my shoulder, ran to his squad car and drove away. He was in a big hurry.

I took Kate's wrist in my hand. Her pulse seemed strong enough. For some reason, she and Tres Munro had been standing yards apart on the patio, a distance that had spared her instant death. Maybe she had walked over to make drinks and she caught only part of the two rounds from the .12-gauge.

They had come gunning for Tres, thinking it was me. They'd thought Kate and I were sitting on the patio by ourselves. Tres's fresh haircut and the new white shirt he was wearing had fooled them. Noah hadn't figured that out yet.

The siren was getting closer now. The rescue squad

truck would be turning into our driveway any second.

Kate was still unconscious and she was bleeding. I leaned down and kissed her softly on her cheek. "For God's sake, don't die," I whispered to her.

Don't die because of me.

I hate hospitals, hate officious nurses even more than I hate those of determined good nature ("It's nice to see that smile this morning"). I hate doctor-gods in hospitals, Guccis and Church's peeking out, hate them even more than hayseed docs, Wallabees on parade. Also, blood tests, salt-free food, the way they wake you up in the middle of the night and the way they make up beds. You hate them until you suddenly have need for expert, concentrated physical care. Then it's funny how quickly a person comes to see hospitals in a different light.

Kate almost died from internal bleeding, but she didn't, thanks to the rescue squad paramedics, who kept her going, and Dr. Angotti, who plucked all the buckshot out of her body and stopped the bleeding.

Dr. Angotti was an old and close friend of Kate's mother, an emergency-room nurse at the hospital until she was killed a few months back in a traffic accident on Route 6, the mid-Cape highway, indeed an accident that happened when she was on her way to the hospital. He had known Kate since she was a child, and he saw that she received the best of care and attention. My own cries and threats no doubt helped a little, but not all that much.

Kate was placed in a room in intensive care after the surgery, and I sat through the hours in a waiting room outside the IC unit, chain-smoked cigarettes I bought from a machine and prayed.

They say most people don't know how much they value something until they've lost it. It's also true that there is nothing a person values more than something he has recovered after he's almost lost it. I can still taste those cigarettes, not my usual brand.

Praying for Kate, I was also praying for myself because I couldn't imagine a life worth living without her. She had saved me from almost certain self-destruction, had given herself to me. At age fifty-one, living with her, joined together, I felt in the middle of life, vibrant, moving forward. Without her, I knew, age would quickly overtake me; it follows you, I was beginning to learn, like a car on a freeway a mile or so behind, coming on slowly but constantly gaining ground. Kate's death would bring it right up on me, soon to pass me by, an old man alone on the road. So I prayed for both of us.

Dr. Angotti assured me after the surgery that Kate was going to recover fully, with a few out-of-sight scars, but she was still under from the shock and the anesthesia, and I was still worried. And as the hours passed I became more and more angry at those who had gunned her down, an anger that I realized was almost beyond control.

So I sat and waited, stewed and worried. Shortly before dawn the IC nurse came out and told me I had a phone call. It was Noah, and he sighed in relief when I told him Kate was going to be okay.

"I checked in a couple of times over the radio," he said. "Still, it's good hearing it from you."

"What about you? Any progress?"

"It's harder than I said. We don't have them. I've got every available policeman on the Cape on it. We have roadblocks on the Bourne and Sagamore bridges, and we've got squad cars checking out every road on the Cape."

"That's a lot of roads."

"Mac, they may have had a boat of some kind. They may have abandoned their car, hidden it somewhere. We're looking."

"Coast Guard?"

"They're alerted. But you know, lots of water out there, not enough Coast Guard, and hundreds of places they could have gone, beyond the bridges. Maybe they had another car waiting. We're still looking."

"I know it's not easy."

"You haven't called the *Globe*, have you? I forgot to tell you not to."

"I got more sense than that."

"Good. We're still keeping it contained, as far as I know. I don't want the bastards keeping check of what we're doing over their car radio."

"I'm not a reporter on this, not right now."

"That's what worries me. I know how you feel. But

don't try to do anything about this on your own. I'm wearing the badge, remember, not you."

I promised Noah I wouldn't do anything, not meaning a word of it, of course.

The nurse came again and told me Kate was conscious and still doing well but, no, absolutely no visitors were allowed in intensive care. Maybe later in the day. Meanwhile, she would convey my regards and continue to keep me informed. After they've taken care of you, it's funny how quickly you start hating hospitals again.

I thought about those two black hoods I had spotted leaving Susan Jacobs's apartment house in Washington. Who had sent them to search that apartment? I thought of Dolph Bridges. People will do a lot, almost anything, to get the chance to run for president. Only the day before, he had offered to make me his campaign press secretary and pay me a lot of money. When I put him off, did I sign my own order of execution? Would Dolph do such a thing? During his years in office had he somehow become associated with organized crime? It was hard to believe. Still, Chicago was in Illinois. I thought about Chicago. There was a pay phone in the hospital waiting room.

I used to buy him lunch now and then. Once, for home protection, he gave me a revolver and I had used it during a moment of temporary madness to threaten the life of my wife, on our final night together. I decided he wouldn't mind an early morning phone call. Hell, cops are used to it.

"I thought you'd run off to the South Seas or something," he said after he answered on the first ring. "What do you want? You must want something, calling so early."

"Bucky, you owe me. All the time I knew you, never once did I call you Frank, neither in print nor behind your back. Never did I write anything about you failing to bring 'em back alive."

"Okay. A little favor."

"You've done a lot of work on organized crime in Chicago. Between us, not for print, did you ever hear Dolph Bridges's name come up?"

"The Senator? Never. Hell, you can quote me on it."

It wasn't the answer I expected to hear and it made me think. "What about a guy named Charls Munro? Big money. Mergers. He's Chicago-based, lives there. Gives a lot of money to charities."

Buck thought for a moment. "Munro?" Then he named a name I had heard of. Often. "Just talk, you know," he said. "Talk of a possible connection, an arrangement. We looked into it. We never could prove anything. You won't be able to, either."

"Thanks, Bucky. I don't have to prove anything in a court of law. I never talked to you," I said. "One more little favor. Look in your book and see if you have an office number for that fine gentleman whose name you mentioned."

Bucky did, and after searching through his book, he gave it to me. I waited until ten o'clock, nine Chicago time.

A lot of Chicago mobsters I've known really dressed like characters in old George Raft movies, but a few of them, after rising to great power over the years through a combination of mayhem and murder, acquire a classy tone. They get bespoke English tailors who fly over from London and fit them in hotel rooms. This one even had a private English secretary.

"Helleow?" he said, answering the phone when I called.

"How ja dew?" he said when I gave him my name and spelled it for him.

"How ja dew," I replied.

"Not heayh. Soddi," he said when I asked to speak to his boss, who used to hang his opponents on meat hooks and watch them squirm to death.

"Eow," I replied. "Please take a message. Quote. I know you are doing it for Munro. Stop it. Close quote. That's all."

"Eow."

"Quite."

"Think yo."

"Think *yo*." I hung up on him.

I sat down again in my waiting-room chair and thought

about Charls Munro. I was remarkably calm, devoid of emotion. My mind was clear as a bell. I decided on a game plan.

I was going to kill the son of a bitch. Let Noah sort it out later.

18

I T WAS A SUNNY, cloudless morning and Helen Bridges
was playing tennis with the young pro. She stopped
the moment she saw me walk out on the patio and came
over.

"Dolph's at the funeral home with Dody Munro.
They're choosing a casket," she told me. She was sweating, breathing heavily, and I didn't ask why she wasn't
there with them. "What a horrible thing to have happened," she did manage to say, as if she had hit the net
with a second serve.

"Obviously they know about their son."

"They flew in from Chicago in their plane the minute
they got the news from the police."

I didn't say anything. I was thinking about Kate, lying
in that hospital bed. I had sent her a dozen roses and a
note, the best I could do, since I was denied permission
to visit her. Through Noah I had caught a ride home in
a Hyannis police car.

"I am sorry about Mrs. Bingham. That is her name?" Helen Bridges said.

"That's correct."

"Look, I have the feeling you don't especially like me."

"Two people have been killed. That's the important thing. And I think you realize all of you are part of it."

"I'm not a murderer, Mr. McFarland."

"I never said you were."

"Nor an accomplice."

"I believe it."

"And neither is Dolph."

"I don't quite believe that. I don't think you do, either. And I think you're afraid this could ruin his chances of being nominated for president. I know how much you want to be First Lady, despite what you say."

"I'd make a fine First Lady, for your information. Better than some others. But don't think it means everything to me."

"I shouldn't be the person telling you this. You know your husband had an affair with Susan Jacobs last summer?"

"I do know that. I've known it for months. Lived with it. I won't lie and say it didn't hurt me."

"He tried to cover up the fact that she worked for a Senate subcommittee he was head of."

"Yes. And I played along with it, reluctantly."

"I'm looking for Charls Munro. Is he with his wife?"

"No. He's looking for you. He was here. He tried to phone you at your home."

"Where'd he go?"

"Over there, I think. I think I see his car. He said to tell you he'd be waiting for you there if you showed up." She pointed across the waters of the Cut to Cranberry House restaurant.

I left Helen Bridges and walked down to the dock. I could see a car in the restaurant's parking lot. It would have taken me half an hour to drive over there, and I was in a hurry. I took off my shirt and trousers and dived into the Cut, into the same cold waters I had gone into Wednesday the week before, led there by my futile search for a wild yellow canary. I swam a little to the left, toward Pilgrim Harbor, because the tide was going out and I could feel it trying to pull me into the sound. Halfway across, I turned over and briefly swam on my back to catch my breath. Helen, I could see, had returned to her tennis game.

I climbed up the ladder and through a broken opening in the railing. Munro had left his car and stood on the deck, watching me swim across. He was waiting for me.

"I need to talk to you," he said to me.

"I'm looking for you, too."

"I want to know what happened last night. I can't find that police chief."

"His name's Noah Simmons, and he's busy looking for

the hit men who killed your son last night thinking he was me."

"It was a mistake."

"Your son was driving the car that went in the water here. The car Susan Jacobs drowned in."

"I understand the local woman you live with was also hit last night."

"Call her Mrs. Bingham. A few hours ago I decided to kill you for what you did, Munro. I still might if you look at me the wrong way, you bastard."

"They were supposed to scare you, that's all. Nobody was supposed to hurt anybody. Somebody screwed up."

"Yes. They killed your only son."

"They've heard from me in no uncertain terms. Tres's death grieves me, of course. Very much. But I couldn't do anything with the boy, try as I might. He was a dope head all his life. His mother couldn't handle him either. I gave up on him."

"Because you were too busy to bother."

"I need to know the circumstances surrounding his death. I've got to explain to his mother."

"The police chief had arrested him for being the driver of the car. Mrs. Bingham was trying to help your boy out. She found him work, tried to get him off drugs. He claimed he had a blackout the night the car went in here. That's why he was at the house. To talk to her. The police chief and I were walking in the yard. It was just the two of them on the patio, with a candle for light. Your gunmen thought your son was me."

"I talked to—to the man I am acquainted with in Chicago. He received your message. So did I. There'll be no repeat."

"That's nice to know."

"I don't want my wife to know what happened last night. She still thinks of him as her baby. She thinks his death was drug-related."

"And you don't want her to know you're responsible for his death."

"Listen, I would've done anything for that kid. College of his choice. Put him in business with me. All he ever wanted to do was ride around on a motorcycle and stick a needle in his arm."

"You remember this. It never would have happened, he'd still be alive, Mrs. Bingham would not have been hurt, if you hadn't caused a couple of killers to take after me."

"It never would have happened if you had listened to reason. You remember that."

"I *did* listen to reason, you stupid ass."

"I'll see to it Mrs. Bingham gets a nice present, a nice ring or something."

"I'm sure she'd appreciate that. She can hold it up and look at it on her finger while she recuperates."

"I said it was a mistake."

"Do you really want to see Dolph Bridges president that badly?"

"I don't mind telling you I want to see him win."

"You'd do anything to see him win. What's in it for you? Defense contracts? Something like that?"

He glared at me. "What kind of a creep do you think I am?" he said.

"A very major creep, one who craves ultimate status. Publicity. Businessman adviser to the president. Your picture in all the magazines, your name in all the gossip columns. All those invitations to state dinners at the White House. Is that worth your son's life, Munro?"

"Did Dolph offer you the job as his news secretary?"

"He did."

"I'll add an extra hundred thousand on the side to the salary."

"Take it and shove it."

"You get this straight. You're not dealing with a crook. I pay my taxes. I'm in *Who's Who*. They profiled me in *Fortune* last year. I'm on every board in Chicago you can name. I didn't have anything to do with the death of that girl, not a thing. Neither did Dolph. I don't want some little something he had nothing to do with spoil his chances."

"You know, with all the nice people in the up-front jobs, I need to keep reminding myself that there are creeps like you around in politics."

No doubt his stare had made many a corporate president shiver. "I don't appreciate that remark," he said.

"Your type is always there. In the background. You always have been and you always will be, no matter what."

"You're right. They shot the wrong man."

I grabbed him by his belt and his shirt collar, hustled him across the deck to the gap in the railing and threw him in the Cut, right where the car had landed.

He made a big splash.

19

NOAH WAS STANDING ON the Munro dock waiting for me when I finished my swim back across the Cut. He didn't mention the dunking I'd given Charls the Second and I decided not to talk about it either. Maybe Noah hadn't seen it or maybe he didn't want to talk about it.

"You'll never make the Olympic swim team. You've got to give up on that old dream." He offered me a hand and hauled me onto the dock. I was too weak to stand up, for a minute or two, until I caught my breath. I'd left Munro floundering in the water.

"You lost them, didn't you," I said, not in condemnation, but as a statement of fact.

"We haven't found them yet. We're still looking."

"They were Munro's boys. He got them from a gang leader in Chicago. They were looking for me, to scare me, he says. They shot the Munro boy by mistake."

"I'm going to get into that, in detail. Katie's out of IC. They told me on the radio. Dede and Bascombe are with her."

That was good news. Noah's strong-willed wife was half his size, no, make that one-third, but her word was law. She and Kate knew and loved each other, had for years. I knew that Dede would take care of her, be sure she had what she needed, and Bascombe would run the errands.

"I've come to talk to Senator Bridges and his people," Noah said. "I called. They're getting together in the house."

"Can I tag along?"

"If they don't protest. And if you'll put on your pants."

"There're a few things I haven't told you about."

"I figured that out. It's why I want you along. Bring them up as they're appropriate."

They were all waiting for us on the air-conditioned sun porch they had turned into a temporary campaign headquarters, Billy Nolan and Thomas Duncan, sitting next to each other on a yellow couch, Eliot More, on the telephone as usual, Helen, sitting quietly in a corner, reading a copy of *Town and Country*, and Dolph, formally dressed in a dark gray lightweight suit. He rose to greet us.

"Dody Munro's resting in an upstairs bedroom," he said. "The doctor's given her a sedative. Should I disturb her?"

"Please, don't," Noah said.

Dolph introduced everybody, casually. "Terrible news about the Munro boy. Cup of coffee, Chief? Mac? You both look like you could use one. I know you've had a tough night." Without saying anything, Eliot, off the phone for a change, walked over to the coffee machine and filled two Styrofoam cups.

"I'll proceed on the assumption you all know about last night," Noah said, accepting the coffee. "I do have a few questions about the night Susan Jacobs died."

"And we're glad to answer them and get this thing cleared up," Dolph said. "I know that Billy Nolan of my staff has told you Miss Jacobs paid us a little surprise visit that night. As he should have. As you might know, she worked on a Senate subcommittee I used to chair. We had no idea she was in the area."

Too casual and friendly, too up front, I decided. Too much. Or was it all in my imagination? I'd find out. I decided to put the ball in play.

"Chief Simmons still doesn't know a few of the details of that evening because I neglected to tell him," I said.

"Christ, here it comes, just like I knew it would," Billy moaned.

"Billy, I want it settled once and for all," Dolph told him.

"And we don't want to see something you had nothing to do with keep you from being elected president of the United States."

"Didn't the Munro boy confess to you that he drove the car into the water?" Eliot More asked Noah.

"He didn't fully confess that. He claimed a loss of memory, a blackout. But I believe that's what happened.

I also think both of them had been using drugs and alcohol," Noah said.

"Just so we understand each other on that point," Eliot said. "There's no question of murder, right? It was an accident, committed by a young man none of us knew."

"It occurs to me, I haven't had a chance to ask the first question yet," Noah said.

Dolph waved his arms up and down. "He's right. Quiet."

"I've said, all I'm trying to do is wrap this thing up," Noah said. "What happened that night after Miss Jacobs left the patio? I understand she simply wandered off, the way she wandered in."

"The steaks were ready. We sat down and ate them," Billy said.

"No talk about Miss Jacobs during the meal? It was a rather bizarre appearance."

"I remember I said maybe she could work for us in New Hampshire," Thomas said. "We all laughed."

"Most of the talk, I remember, was about the reason for the party," Eliot said. "Senator Lifsey had come over to our side. That was a big victory for us. Thomas, I remember, had us all laughing with an imitation of him he does."

"She called you a cool brown dude when she first arrived, didn't she, Thomas? Something like that. And Billy Nolan said you were talking with her when he went

247

to get her a drink. Did she tell you where she was living in North Walpole, in the Cranberry House, just across the Cut?"

"At that point, I don't think she knew where she was living at," Thomas said.

"What about you, Miss More? As I recall, you told her to call *you* about a campaign job. You had no way of knowing where she was staying in town?"

"Correct."

"You see, it occurred to me, well, who among you knew she was living right across the Cut from the house where you all were staying?"

All of them were suddenly wary of this small-town policeman and his questions. I could sense it. My turn to throw a bomb.

"Susan Jacobs walked over and gave Dolph a hug and a kiss, according to Billy Nolan. She promised him full support and cooperation and said she wouldn't go around shooting her mouth off," I said. "Because Dolph was banging her last summer in Washington while his wife was out of town."

Helen closed her *Town and Country*. "She said nothing to me that night, introduced herself and shook my hand very quickly, that's all."

"The same with the Munros, I gather," Noah said.

"But, according to Billy, she hugged Dolph and whispered sweet nothings in his ear. That's the other thing I hadn't told you," I said.

248

Noah nodded, as if I had told him something he had long suspected. "Mrs. Bridges, did you know who she was that night?"

"Oh, yes." A little bitter, I thought.

"You knew about their affair last summer?"

"All about it. For a long time."

"Didn't you ask your husband about her later that night? It's only human. Didn't you wonder what she was doing here in North Walpole? It's an unlikely coincidence, showing up in the same little Cape Cod village."

"Yes. I asked him about her that night, when we were in bed."

"What did he tell you?"

"I told her the truth, that I had no idea why Susan Jacobs was here," Dolph said.

"What is this? The Grand Inquisition?" Eliot shouted. "This man was a United States senator."

"Whatever she whispered in your ear worried you," Helen said calmly to Dolph, as if the rest of us weren't there. "After you thought I was asleep, and I almost was, you slipped out of bed and left the bedroom."

Helen hadn't forgiven him his infidelity, I decided. She thought about it a lot.

"I couldn't sleep," Dolph said. "I walked around in the yard."

"Did any of the rest of you see the Senator?" Noah asked. "Miss More? Mr. Nolan? Mr. Duncan?"

"No comment," Thomas said.

"This isn't a post-game interview," I said to him. "It's a police interrogation. Answer the chief."

"No comment," Thomas said again.

"Christ! Get off his back," Billy shouted.

I remembered something. Funny how things pop into your mind. "Thomas Duncan doesn't lie," I told Noah. "He was the only child of a very religious woman and he promised her when she was on her deathbed he'd never tell a lie. And he never has. Billy wrote about it in an old *Sports Illustrated* article I remember reading. That's why he doesn't want to answer your question."

Thomas was gazing up at the ceiling of the sun porch, either looking at the angel of truth circling happily over his head or watching his Washington future fly away.

"Did you see the Senator that night?" Noah asked him.

"Billy, he must have drunk fifteen beers that night," Thomas said. "That many beers makes him snore. We were sleeping in the guest room over the garage to make room for Mr. and Mrs. Munro. Billy, he woke me up with his snoring. Sounded like a war going on. I got up and stood on the balcony."

"And you saw Senator Bridges. What did he do?" Noah asked.

"Dolph, he came out and got in the Jeep and drove away," Thomas said.

"And Tres saw his car lights at the restaurant," I said to Noah.

"Now, wait a minute. Just hold on a minute," Eliot More said forcefully.

"When Susan Jacobs was whispering in your ear, I don't think it was sweet nothings or further promises of her silence. I think she was telling you she lived at the restaurant across the Cut, in the bunkroom upstairs," I said to Dolph. "And you wondered why. Had she come here to cause you trouble, despite what she said? To blackmail you? You didn't know. So you went over to the restaurant to try and find out."

"Shut your mouth. You're not the law," Eliot said to me.

Hell, I knew that, but Noah didn't stop me, so I continued. I had been lied to, led astray, offered a bribe. My woman had been wounded and I might have been killed. I was mad as hell.

"I don't know what you found there or what you did there, if the car was in the water or you drove it in. But you were there, Dolph," I said to him.

"Bullshit!" Eliot shouted. "He's guessing," she said to Noah.

"No, it's not called bullshit," Noah said. "It might be called leaving the scene of an accident. That's against the law in the Commonwealth of Massachusetts."

"You're trying to get your name in the papers."

"I know I'd be accused of that," Noah said.

"You're damned right you would be."

"Not in anything I write," I said.

251

Eliot ignored me and continued to talk to Noah. "You might as well take out that pistol and shoot him," she said.

"Miss More, I have no choice."

"The hell you don't. You can't tell me you have to get into that leaving-the-scene-of-an-accident bullshit. Even if it's true, which it's not."

"I have got to take this to the district attorney. Somebody's been murdered in cold blood, remember. I've got to. And he'll ask the district judge to order inquests on both Susan Jacobs and Tres Munro. That's all there is to it."

"Chappaquiddick! It'll be exactly the same."

"I hope not. I don't want that."

"Want it or not, that's what we'll be in for. With reporters and photographers coming out of the woodwork, and with everybody holier-than-thou. Look at McFarland. He's so anxious right now to get to a telephone he's almost foaming at the mouth."

"Noah's only doing his duty. I'm only trying to do my job," I said.

"McFarland, you know as well as I do what will happen in this little town. It'll be a madhouse. And Dolph will be ruined. He might as well take himself out of the race right now, this very minute."

"I didn't do anything to cause this. Neither did Noah."

"You'll both profit from it, in different ways. You were on your last legs, McFarland."

"I'm going to write it straight, if that makes any difference to you. No speculation, no suggestions. A fair shake."

"It doesn't matter how you write it, and you know it. Not one damn bit. Every paper, every magazine and, God knows, every television network will send their own people up here, trying to find more. Searching for scandal. That's the name of the game today."

"I don't like it but I can't help it."

"You know that's what we're trying so hard to prevent. Open house. A red-meat feast for media mad dogs."

"Eliot, it's going to come out. Nothing can stop it now."

"Excuse me, Helen, but what we're talking about here is, Dolph had a little slip last summer with that girl," Billy said.

"And I know the details," I said.

"Exactly. If you found them so easy, you can bet your ass every other reporter in Washington will find them, too, once it's known that they exist. Find them and print them."

"And good-bye, presidential campaign," Eliot said.

"And there'll be lots of editorials condemning the publication of the details, printing them again, of course. *That's* the name of the game today. It didn't used to be that way. Fucking for fun, people turned their heads. Otherwise, we wouldn't have had any candidates. You played that game, Mac."

253

"Yes. That doesn't mean it was a good game."

"Some good people got elected."

"That's the point," Thomas said. "A lot of people want to see this man here elected president. Lots of people think he's the best man for the job, a little messing around or not. I'm one of them."

"And how many of the other candidates in this race could stand to have all their closet doors opened?" Eliot asked.

"Special rules for special people. That's what you're all saying," I told them.

"No. Fair play. Realistic rules," Eliot said.

"It doesn't seem like real people are getting much to say in this," Thomas said.

"Every time you try to cover something up in politics, it comes out looking even worse than it is," I said.

"Unless you get away with it," Dolph said. "I'm probably going to be forced to drop out of the race by all this. But, remember, if you get away with it, then it never comes out at all. *That's* the name of the game. Don't get caught."

"I realize you believe that, Dolph," I said. "But, you know, a guy screws up now and again, gets caught off-base, people say he's only human, if he's a basically decent person. It shows through. And no matter how much a person tries to hide it and cover it up, if he's an unprincipled son of a bitch down deep, that eventually shows through, too. So don't kid yourself. You would have gotten caught, sooner or later."

"All this talk doesn't matter one way or the other," Noah said. "I'm an officer of the law and I've got my duty to perform. An official public investigation is called for here."

Helen sighed. "Politics *is* a dirty business, isn't it, darling," she said sweetly to her husband.

20

"**D**ON'T YOU DARE REFER to me using the *A* word," the lawyer Bascombe Midgeley said indignantly to the Full Cleveland.

"Asshole!" he shouted.

"All we need. A brawl in the hospital waiting room," Noah said to me as we left the elevator and came upon the two of them having it out.

"Ah! *Chief*," Bascombe said, spotting Noah and pretending he didn't know him. "Perhaps *you* can assist with this person. A uniformed officer of the law might well be what's needed in this situation."

"What's the problem?"

"This *asshole* tried to stop the orderlies from putting my wife in her hospital room who has a broken leg is the problem!" shouted the Full Cleveland. "And now I found him talking to the head nurse, trying to get her moved out."

He was wearing a lime-green polyester sports jacket, vivid plaid polyester trousers, a white belt and white

patent leather leisure shoes. A Full Cleveland such out-
fits are called in some Chicago circles.

"Holding the fort. It's a double. No private rooms are
available yet," Bascombe explained to us. "Come on,
Mac. Kate's woozy but she's doing fine and she's been
asking for you. Dede's with her." He took my arm and
led me down the corridor. Noah followed. He and I had
driven to the Hyannis hospital in separate cars directly
from the house at the Cut when we left Dolph Bridges.

Kate was wearing a hospital gown and she looked weak
and white-faced, but she had a faint smile for me when
I entered her room and went through the curtain that
divided it into a double. My roses were on the window-
sill, and Dede, a welcome sight, was hovering over her.

I kissed Kate on her cheek and sat in a chair beside her
bed. "Please don't try to talk unless you find it absolutely
necessary to tell me you love me as much as I love you,"
I said. "It's okay just to nod your head yes. Do you think
you'll feel up to getting home and cooking supper tonight? If you don't, say so. I'll pick up something at
Burger Chef."

"Kate's still a little out of it, but she knows she was shot
and she knows the Munro boy's dead," Dede said. "She's
not supposed to talk or move and you guys are not supposed to hang around very long. I'm staying. There's
supper in the freezer you can microwave later for you
and Mac, Noah."

"From the *Midwest*, are you?" we heard a calmer Bascombe, now on a more diplomatic tack, say to the polyes-

ter man on the other side of the closed curtain. "We certainly aren't trying to force your lovely wife out on the street, old cock. Not with that huge cast on her leg. I was thinking perhaps a much larger double room she could share with someone, that's all. Maybe a better view for her, on the window side. I'll have a word with admissions about it."

"Noah's got the dart board at the Binnacle booked for us next week," I told Kate.

"Katie, we'll kill them, as usual," Noah said.

"Don't use that word," I said, still looking at Kate. "I see the flowers arrived. Good. Nice roses, if I do say so myself. I figure a couple of Band-Aids here and there and you'll be as good as new in a day or so. God, you're beautiful."

"You'll find Hyannis an interesting town," we heard Bascombe tell the tourist man. "There are quite a number of first-rate men's clothing shops here, for example."

"MouMou says to say hello and tell you she wants you home as soon as possible."

There was a tear in Kate's eye.

"Don't worry about that damn dog," I told her.

"You guys get out of here," Dede said. She led her husband and me outside, her arms around our waists. Bascombe was still working on the polyester man.

"God, I've been worried to death about her," I told Dede. "See, my idea was to be light and humorous and not let her see how concerned I was."

Dede kissed me on my cheek. "I'm sure Kate under-stands. Mac, I wouldn't lose sleep over that."

"I've got work to do," Noah said. "I've got to talk with the district attorney, lay it all out, including Dolph Bridges and Charls Munro."

"And I've got to call the *Globe*."

Noah and I left Dede to look after Kate and walked to the waiting room.

"You know, my father was a commercial fisherman, and, I was thinking, he would have made a pretty good president," Noah said to me. "He was a nice-looking guy, friendly, lots of energy. He had plenty of common sense. He didn't screw around. He was honest, said what he thought. And he knew the difference between right and wrong. Hell, it doesn't take a genius to be president of the United States."

I had work to do. The moment Noah entered the ele-vator, I picked up the pay telephone and used my credit card to call the Boston *Globe*.

The Front Page, name it, in nearly every old movie or play I ever saw about newspapering, at its dramatic con-clusion the excited reporter, notebook in hand, press card stuck in the ribbon of his hat, and scoop in sole possession, yells it. Twenty-five years the real thing and never before did I have the chance. Now I did.

"Hello, sweetheart," I told the *Globe* operator. "Give me rewrite."

DOUGLAS KIKER is one of the nation's best-known and most widely respected television news correspondents. As a reporter for the *Atlanta Journal,* he observed the turmoil of the Southern civil rights movement. As White House correspondent for the *New York Herald Tribune,* he was present in Dallas when President Kennedy was killed. As an NBC News correspondent, he has covered every national political convention since 1964. He reported for NBC News from Vietnam, Northern Ireland, the Middle East, and, on special assignment, the revolution in Iran. For his reports on the Jordan war, in 1970, he was awarded broadcasting's most coveted prize, the George Foster Peabody Award. He is the author of two novels, *The Southerner* and *Strangers on the Shore,* as well as *Murder on Clam Pond,* an earlier mystery about Mac McFarland. His articles and short stories have appeared in the *Atlantic Monthly, Harper's,* and the *Yale Review,* among other publications.